He didn't want to play it safe now.

Dave slipped his arms around Kara and drew her to him ever so carefully, a nurseryman with a new cactus he was still trying to determine how best to handle without getting pierced.

"I remember," he replied, his voice low, his mind already trying to figure out how to survive the turbulent ride looming ahead.

Part of him was fervently hoping that the impact of that first kiss had been, for some unknown reason, all in his imagination.

Part of him was hoping it hadn't been.

Dear Reader,

People are always asking me where I get my ideas for stories. Most of the time they are knitted together from bits and pieces that come from newspapers, magazine interviews, TV shows and conversations around me. It's usually hard to trace an idea back to its origin. That's not the case this time. This story has its roots in handwritten letters, then typed ones and finally emails, all of which have spanned the last thirty-plus years.

I first met Nancy, my oldest young friend, in third grade. She was poised and pretty and I idolized her. Slowly, because I was shy back then, we became friends. We never stopped. I moved to California, she remained in New York. We wrote sporadically. And then we both became mothers at the same time. She had a son, I had a daughter. Hers was born in April, mine in July. And over the years, one or the other of us has wistfully said, "What if—?" Luckily, from our kids' point of view, there is not a chance in the world that our wistfulness will bear fruit, since three thousand miles divide the two homes. So I did the next best thing. I imagined it on paper. And hopefully, you will be entertained (and for the record, if you're wondering, neither one of us is going to tell our kids about this book).

Thank you for reading and, as ever, I wish you someone to love who loves you back.

Best,

Marie Ferrarella

THE LAST
FIRST KISS

MARIE FERRARELLA

Harlequin®

SPECIAL EDITION

Recycling programs
for this product may
not exist in your area.

ISBN-13: 978-0-373-65657-8

THE LAST FIRST KISS

MARIE FERRARELLA

This *USA TODAY* bestselling and RITA® Award-winning author has written more than two hundred books for Harlequin Books and Silhouette Books, some under the name Marie Nicole. Her romances are beloved by fans worldwide. Visit her website, www.marieferrarella.com.

To
Nancy Parodi Neubert,
My Youngest Oldest Friend

Chapter One

"Oh, c'mon, Lisa, think about it. What have we got to lose?"

Maturity, for the most part, had been kind to Paulette Calhoun, leaving few of the customary telltale age lines on her face. Closing in on sixty, the tastefully dressed strawberry blonde with deep blue eyes leaned her still very trim body in, as if the proximity would add more weight to her urgings and win the other woman over.

Lisa Scarlatti, younger by three months, sat facing her lifelong friend across a black lacquer-top table for two. She held a cup of tea between her hands, the warmth just beginning to fade.

"Well, offhand, I'd say our kids. If Dave so much as smells a romantic setup, quiet though he normally is, he'll read me the riot act. And, if memory serves, I'm pretty sure that goes double for your independent, outspoken Kara."

Laughter sparkled in Paulette's eyes. "They won't smell a setup because they know that *we* know better than to try one, which is the beauty of all this."

Lisa frowned. Her heart fought with her brain. Since they lived a good sixty miles apart, she and Paulette got together for lunch several times a year. More often now that they both found themselves unavoidably and sadly unattached. Paulette's husband had died almost thirteen years ago, while Lisa's had passed away after an accident eight years ago.

"I never thought of alienating my child as having anything to do with beauty," she told Paulette. "For heaven's sake, Thomas and I put that boy through medical school. I'm finally coming out from under that staggering debt. Let me enjoy Dave for five minutes before I do something that will have him renouncing me in the public square."

Paulette rolled her eyes. "And here I thought I was the dramatic one. Dave's not going to renounce you," she insisted. The subject of setting up their children had been on her mind ever since she'd heard about her second cousin's overwhelming success in playing matchmaker for not just her daughter, but her friends' daughters—and son—as well. Hell, if Maizie could do it, she could, too. And so could Lisa.

"Listen, this plan is perfect," Paulette enthused. "You said your niece's little boy has a birthday coming up, right?"

There was a trap here somewhere. Lisa knew Paulette too well for there not to be. "Right," she replied cautiously.

"And what, according to you, does Melissa's adorable son, Ryan, want more than anything in the whole world for his birthday?"

Lisa sighed. She saw where this was going.

"'The Kalico Kid' video game," Lisa finally said because Paulette was obviously waiting.

Nodding, Paulette asked, "And what is impossible to get?"

Why were they playing this game? "'The Kalico Kid' video game."

Paulette's wide smile grew wider. "And where does my daughter work?"

Lisa closed her eyes. She was being sucked into this, but there was no other course open to her. "At the video game company that puts out 'The Kalico Kid.'"

"Exactly," Paulette declared with feeling, warming to her subject. "So, since Dave is a softhearted sweetheart who likes making his cousin's little boy happy, and Kara has access to copies of the all-but-impossible-to-get game, it's all very simple." She paused for a moment for effect, then delivered her plan's grand finale. "I ask Kara to get a copy and deliver it to Dave when he's volunteering at that free clinic near where Kara works—"

"And just like that—" Lisa snapped her fingers, a touch of uncustomary sarcasm in her voice "—they'll see each other, and angels will sing while the sound of heavenly music echoes everywhere."

"No." Paulette dismissed her friend's convoluted scenario. "Dave'll be grateful and offer to take Kara out to dinner to repay her for her kindness. You raised a very polite son, Lisa." Paulette folded her hands before the still half-full teacup. "And then they can take it from there."

"Maybe there'll be no place to take it," Lisa suggested.

She knew how stubborn her son could be. He hadn't told her anything close to personal in more than ten years. The only way she deduced that he was unattached was that he kept coming back to his childhood home on his days off. Much as she loved seeing him, she wanted him to spend his days off with a woman worthy of him, nurturing a relationship.

"At least we would have tried," Paulette insisted. She attempted another tactic. Putting her hand on top of her friend's, she peered up at her, a silent plea in her eyes. "Don't you remember how we used to all go on family vacations together when our husbands were alive, just the six of us? And you and I used to watch the kids play and dream about Dave and Kara getting married?"

"We used to watch them fight," Lisa corrected. "And anyway, that was a long time ago. It hasn't been the six of us for a while now," she reminded Paulette. "Thomas and Neil aren't around any longer." The words weighed heavily on her tongue. All these years later, she still missed Thomas as if he'd died yesterday. She doubted that the ache would ever really go away.

"All the more reason to get our kids together," Paulette pressed. "Neither one of them is getting any younger, you know."

Lisa pointed out one glaring fact. "It's not like we haven't tried before."

More than once they had attempted to get their grown offspring together, but something always came up at the last minute, preventing it. It had been *years* since Kara and Dave were even close to being in the same room at the same time.

Paulette waved her hand, dismissing the argument as not worth her time or effort to get into.

"That was for occasions—Christmas, Thanksgiving," she specified. "One or the other always begged off, saying they had to work. I swear Kara logs in more overtime than any other human being on the face of the earth, with the possible exception of Dave. You ask me, they're perfect for each other. All we need to do is get them to see that."

Paulette beamed at her friend. "There was no pressure before. We kept it light. But this time, I mean business," she announced. "This is going to be more like a sneak attack." Her eyes glowed with anticipation. "They'll never know what hit them."

Lisa still didn't like it. She enjoyed the relationship she had with her son. They didn't speak as much as she'd like, but he did call her and he appeared on her doorstep on many of his days off, which were rare. She treasured that and didn't want anything to jeopardize their relationship.

"But we'll definitely know what hit us," she countered.

Paulette stared at the friend she'd had for more than five decades. "Since when have you gotten so negative?"

Lisa shrugged. Then, because once again Paulette was waiting for an answer, she tried to explain.

"If we don't try to get Dave and Kara together, I can always hope that someday it'll happen. If we do get them together and it blows up in our faces, then it's all over. The dream is gone. For good. I'd rather have a piece of a warm, fuzzy dream than a chunk of stone-cold negative reality."

Paulette summoned a look of complete disappointment. "The Lisa I knew and went to school with was absolutely fearless. Where did she go? What happened to her?"

"The Lisa you knew was a lot younger. I like peace and quiet these days. And a son who calls his mother once in a while."

The sigh that escaped Paulette's lips could have rivaled a Louisiana hurricane. "So you're not going to ask Kara if she can get that game from her company for Dave so that he can give it to Ryan?"

Lisa's frown deepened several degrees. She knew when she was outmatched. Paulette could wield guilt like a finely honed weapon. "I hate it when you put on that long face."

The long face was instantly gone, replaced by a wide smile of satisfaction. "I know."

It was Lisa's turn to sigh. "I think if anyone should do the asking, it should be you. Otherwise, Kara's going to be suspicious. I don't call her," she pointed out. "So getting a call from me might alert her that we're up to something. In any event, this'll make it your fault when Dave and Kara decide to put us out to sea on a tiny ice floe."

"They'll have to interact with each other in order to do that," Paulette concluded, grinning. "So, either way, it's a win-win scenario. Okay, that's settled," she declared happily, adding, "Suddenly, I feel very hungry." She picked up the menu.

Lisa's eyes narrowed as she looked at her best friend. She'd walked right into that one, she thought. "Suddenly," she countered, "I'm not."

Paulette raised her blue eyes to Lisa's face. "Eat. You're going to need your strength."

Which was exactly what Lisa was afraid of.

Something was off in the universe. She could just *feel* it.

Closing her eyes and taking a five-second break, Kara Calhoun, senior quality assurance engineer for Dynamic Video Games, tried to tell herself that she was allowing the game she'd been assigned to crack to get to her.

After working on this particular version, with its wizards, warriors and spell-casting witches, for close to twenty days straight—not counting the overtime she'd been forced to amass—Kara was beginning to feel as if she had become one with the game. Not exactly something she'd recommend to anyone wanting to maintain their hold on reality.

Luckily, her hold on reality was stronger than most. She'd loved video games ever since she'd wandered into her very first arcade at the age of four, when she'd become hooked on the whirling lights and noises. But most of all, she loved the challenge of defeating whatever adversary she found herself pitted against.

Even so, she was careful to keep it all in perspective. These were games she was working with and playing with, nothing more. In no manner, shape or form did they remotely represent real life.

Definitely not hers.

There was no way she was going to allow what happened to her coworker Jeffrey Allen to happen to her. He began believing that the people within his game were communicating with him, warning him of some imminent disaster. He'd clearly lost his grip on reality.

That being said, she couldn't shake the feeling that there really was something off. That some sort of pending doom was shimmering on the horizon and it had her name written all over it.

Maybe she needed a vacation, Kara thought.

She began to play again and immediately discovered another glitch in the program. The Black Knight was not supposed to be able to ride his equally dark steed into the ocean, much less have the horse gallop *across* the waves.

Kara shook her head. It seemed that every time she pointed out one error and the programmers fixed it, two more errors would pop up, tossing another wrench into the works. To make matters worse, the company's deadline was swiftly approaching, and she was beginning to have serious doubts that the game would be ready to hit the stores as had been promised.

But, ready or not, here it came, Kara thought, knowing how the market operated. Games were often sent out without having all their programming problems and bugs addressed with the fervent hope that the buyers wouldn't find the glitches. Right. And maybe pigs would fly.

When the phone rang on her desk, Kara debated

simply ignoring it. After all, she was deeply involved in trying to figure out exactly why the knight's horse was veering off its path. Preferably before six o'clock tonight. The idea of actually getting home by something resembling normal time for a change seemed like a borderline miracle to her.

The phone continued to ring. Kara shot it a dirty look and sighed. With her luck, it was probably someone from Corporate calling, and she knew they would only go on calling until she finally picked up.

Might as well stop putting off the inevitable, she thought. Muttering an oath, she yanked the receiver from its cradle. "This is Kara. Speak."

"My God, is that the way you answer the phone at work?"

"Hello, Mother." Kara immediately thought of her feeling that something was off. Maybe there was something to this intuition stuff after all. "What can I do for you? Speak fast, I'm up against a deadline."

She heard her mother make a noise and could just envision the disapproving look that came over the woman's heart-shaped face.

"You're always up against deadlines. That's all I ever hear. I never see you anymore, Kara," her mother complained.

Pointing out that, yes, she did, would do her no good and Kara knew it. "Get out the pictures you insisted on taking at Easter and look at them, Mom. I haven't changed any since then."

"You still haven't gained any weight?" Paulette lamented.

Trust her mother to turn her remark against her. "That's a good thing, Mother."

Unable to concentrate on two things at once when one of those things involved her mother, Kara stopped working on the game and turned away from the monitor. She lowered her voice. This was not a conversation she wanted anyone in one of the other cubicles to overhear.

"Are you actually calling me to find out if I'm eating?"

"No, I'm calling to ask you a favor. Your company puts out that 'Kalico Kid' video game, doesn't it?"

This was a trap of some sort, she could smell it. "You know we do," Kara answered cautiously. She'd mentioned how hard her team had worked on getting the game out on time. What was her mother up to?

"Can you get a copy?"

The company store had several copies set aside. "I probably can," she allowed, "seeing as how I worked on it for six months." Kara sat up, her body at attention. "Don't tell me you've suddenly decided to play video games." Mentally, she crossed her fingers. It would be nice if her mother found another hobby other than watching over her life, Kara thought. She also knew that the chances of that happening were as unlikely as her striking gold in the company's first-floor ladies' room.

"Lisa's son, Dave, needs to get his hands on a copy for his cousin's little boy. It's a birthday party and Ryan, Melissa's son—Melissa is his—"

"I get it, Mom, I get it," Kara protested, trying to

stop her mother before the woman verbally drew an elaborate family tree for her.

"Anyway, Ryan has his little heart set on getting that game. Can you come through with one, or is he going to be heartbroken for his birthday?" her mother asked her bluntly.

No doubt about it, when it came to wielding guilt, her mother knew no equal. "Stop, Mom," Kara pleaded, holding the receiver away from her ear. "I'll see what I can do." Pulling her calendar over, she picked up a pen, intending to mark the date. "When do you need it by?"

"Tomorrow."

"Tomorrow?" Kara echoed. Talk about being last minute. "Mother, that's—" She stopped herself. She knew better than to attempt to argue with the woman who'd made it into an art form. Instead, she said, "I'll see what I can do, Mom."

"That's my girl." Warmth radiated from the phrase. "I told Lisa you'd come through. By the way, would you mind dropping it off with Dave when you get it? Tomorrow is his day to work at the Seventeenth Street Clinic. He volunteers there, you know."

As if her mother hadn't already told her that little tidbit countless number of times. "You don't say."

"The clinic isn't all that far from you," Paulette went on, ignoring the sarcasm in her daughter's voice.

Kara suppressed a sigh. If she sighed too often, she was going to wind up hyperventilating. Worse, she'd have her mother fussing over her, which was the last thing she needed.

"I know where Seventeenth Street is, Mother." This time, a hint of impatience came through.

Sadly, it appeared that her mother hadn't perceived it. "Wonderful, then we're all set. Dave'll be there all day," Paulette stressed. "That young man is positively selfless, never takes any time off for himself," Paulette marveled.

This was getting a little too thick. Kara smelled a rat—the kind that wore high heels and was given to being sneaky.

"Mother—"

"Oops," Paulette exclaimed abruptly. "I've got to go. Talk to you later, Kara. Bye!"

Her mother's flood of words came at her fast and furious—just before the receiver on the other end went "click."

She'd been right, Kara thought as she leaned forward and replaced the receiver into its cradle. The universe was out of whack today. Now all she had to do was figure out why.

There were times, like today, when Dr. David Scarlatti wished he'd been blessed with an extra set of hands. Either that, or had learned to increase his energy level and work twice as fast as he normally did. There just never seemed to be enough hours in the day for him to do everything he needed to.

That was especially true whenever he volunteered at the free clinic. He'd been here since seven and he didn't feel as if he was making a dent. For every patient he saw, two more seemed to pop up to take his or her place. After six hours straight, the waiting room was *still* jammed. So much so that some of the patients were sitting cross-legged on the floor.

Nobody was here for something as mundane as a routine checkup. Everyone had something wrong, usually something that they had been enduring for at least several weeks before grudgingly swallowing their pride and making the pilgrimage to the clinic.

It was one o'clock. Typically, most doctors' offices were closed for lunch at this hour. But for him, lunch was only a faraway dream. Other than a candy bar, he hadn't had anything to eat—nor the time to consume it if he'd thought to bring something with him.

He didn't like being hungry, but they were down one doctor today, which made him not low man on the totem pole but *sole* man on the totem pole. Added to that, one of the nurses didn't show and the one who did looked as if she were running on empty. Clarice, a normally no-nonsense nurse whose age he wouldn't dare attempt to guess—he knew she had grandchildren—had been out sick for a week, and it was rather obvious to him that she needed a couple more days.

Too bad neither he nor the clinic had that kind of luxury. There were patients to attend to, and there was no putting that on hold.

As Dave walked out Mrs. Rayburn and her allergy-challenged twins, Megan and Moira, he paused by the reception desk to pick up the next file. There had to be a break coming soon, right?

"How many more, Clarice?" he asked the full-figured dynamo, who was, among other things, his first line of defense.

"You don't want to know," the woman informed him darkly.

Since the clinic had originally opened its doors, Clarice Sanchez had seen doctors come, burn out and go. For reasons he wasn't quite sure of but was eternally grateful for, after an initial butting of heads, the somber nurse had taken him under her large, protective wing. Clarice was the one who kept things moving, even when she was operating at less than her usual maximum efficiency.

Dave read the side of the folder and was about to call the name of his next patient when suddenly, someone was calling out his instead.

"Dave!"

Caught off guard, he momentarily forgot about Ramon Mendoza and glanced about the waiting area to see who had just addressed him by his first name. No one did that around here. It was disrespectful. If they spoke to him, they always invoked his title in a grateful voice.

He didn't have far to look. His line of sight was immediately engaged by a vaguely familiar, rather sexy-looking blonde. She was striding across the packed room, heading toward him as if she were the bullet and he was the bull's-eye. From the expression on her face, he could see that she seemed agitated.

One thing was for damn sure. She certainly didn't look as if she belonged here. It was like a lily suddenly sprouting in the middle of a field of weeds.

Before he could acknowledge the woman—God, that face looked familiar—Clarice stepped in. "I already told you," she snapped at the blonde, giving her a withering look, "you're gonna have to wait your turn, lady."

"I just need to see the doctor for a minute," the blonde insisted.

"That's what everyone says," Clarice told her coldly. "Now either sit down and wait your turn or I'm going to get someone to escort you out of here."

Kara decided that she was going to give this one more try and then leave. Lunch was almost over and she was hungry. More to the point, she really didn't need this kind of abuse.

"Dave," she called to him again, deliberately ignoring his guard dragon. "It's Kara Calhoun. Your mother sent me."

Chapter Two

Dave found himself staring at the blonde, stunned. While the face was vaguely familiar in a distant sort of way, the name was familiar in a far more vivid, in-your-face kind of fashion.

He knew only one Kara, God help him.

That would be the only daughter of his mother's oldest friend, Paulette Calhoun. Every single memory associated with Kara Calhoun was fraught with either embarrassment or frustrated annoyance—or both. He didn't even try to remember one good moment spent in her company. There weren't any.

Back when he was a little boy, his parents and hers would get together frequently. All the summer vacation memories of his childhood had Kara in them. Kara and turmoil. He'd been rather shy and introverted. Two years younger, Kara had been the exact opposite, as wild as a hurricane, and just as fearless. He'd felt inadequate.

And then mercifully, just before he turned thirteen, his father's company began moving him, and thus them, from location to location. They traversed the Northwest and then the Southwest. Changing addresses so frequently made it hard for him to make any friends, but the upside was that at least during the rest of the year, he didn't have to spend time confined in some remote summerhouse with the wild tomboy, counting the hours until September and the beginning of school.

If, after all these years, this gorgeous woman really *was* Kara Calhoun, then God, he couldn't help thinking, had a very macabre and somewhat sadistic sense of humor.

Despite the pressures generated by an incredibly hectic morning stapled to the makings of an equally insane afternoon, Dave stopped what he was doing and waved his next patient into the first open room.

"Be right there, Mr. Mendoza," he promised.

Then, instead of following the man, Dave rounded the reception desk and walked toward the sexy-looking blonde with the long legs.

That just *couldn't* be Kara.

Still, why would she say she was if she wasn't? He wasn't going to have any peace until he found out for certain one way or the other, so, warily, he asked, "Kara?"

"Yes," she cried with the same sort of feeling a contestant might display when their partner finally guessed the right answer after being supplied with countless clues.

He still couldn't get himself to believe it. Why, after all these years, would she suddenly appear here, in a place where she was clearly out of her element? Her shoes alone looked as if they might equal a week's salary for one of his patients—the ones who actually *had* a job.

"Kara Calhoun," he said, trying to reconcile the image of a bratty, skinny girl with pigtails and a nasty sense of humor with the clearly gorgeous young woman who was standing in the packed waiting room. Obviously nature could work miracles.

Why all the drama? Kara wondered. The Dave she remembered had been a super-brainy geek. Had he been forced to trade in his brains for looks? Was that how it worked?

"Want to see my driver's license?" she offered, wondering what it would take to convince this man who she was.

The touch of sarcasm in her voice was all he needed to convince him. "It's you, all right. Still have the sunny disposition of an armadillo, I see."

She stretched her lips back in an obviously forced smile. "You've filled out since I last saw you." Which, she added silently, was putting it mildly. If the way his lab coat fit was any indication, the man now had muscles instead of arms that could have doubled for toothpicks. "Too bad your personality didn't want to keep up."

He would have liked nothing better than to turn his back on her and walk away, but she hadn't just appeared here like some directionally challenged genie out of a bottle. There was a reason Kara had sought him out after all these years and he had just enough curiosity to wonder why.

He made it simple for her. He asked. "What are you doing here?"

"I was wondering the same thing myself," she cracked. But then, as he apparently lost patience and began to turn on his heel to walk away, she relented. There was no point in coming all the way over here and *not* giving him the game. "I brought you a copy of the latest version of 'The Kalico Kid' video game. Your mother told mine that your cousin's little boy's birthday is coming up and he's dying to get his hands on one."

If this were anyone else, he would have expressed his gratitude, paid for the game and taken it. But this was Kara, and the ordinary rules didn't apply here. His memory was crowded with a host of different sneaky tricks that a gangly ten-year-old played on his trusting twelve-year-old body. Spending summers trapped in her company had taught him to hold everything she was involved in suspect.

His eyes narrowed as he looked at her. Motioning her closer to create at least a semblance of privacy, he asked, "What's the catch?"

"Catch?" Boy, talk about not being trusting. But then, looking back, maybe she couldn't quite blame him. She had been pretty hard on Dave when they were kids. "The catch is you have to spin a room full of straw into gold by morning."

"You can do that?" a small voice directly behind her piped up. Despite the distance, her voice had carried enough so that the only child in the room heard, and he was clearly awestruck.

Kara turned around to see a little boy of about eight or ten. He looked rather small and fragile, so he might have even been older. She couldn't tell for sure. But she did know that he had the widest smile she'd ever seen.

He also, she noted, had an extremely pale complexion and, despite the fact that it was unseasonably hot outside, he was wearing a bright blue wool cap pulled down low on his head. She suspected that the boy's mother, sitting behind him, had put it on him to keep people from staring. The stigma of a bald head on one so young was difficult to cope with.

"She was making a joke, Gary," Dave told the boy. "She does that kind of thing."

Or did, he added silently. The truth was that he had no way of knowing what Kara was like these days, but he suspected she was still true to form—even if her outer form had turned out incredibly well.

He got back to business. "How much do I owe you for 'The Kalico Kid' game?"

But Kara was no longer paying attention to him. Her attention was now completely focused on the little boy. Even if he hadn't been the only child in the room, he would have stood out because of his near-ghostly pallor.

"You really have 'The Kalico Kid' game?" Gary asked. She would have had to be blind not to notice the wistful gleam that came into his brown eyes.

She smiled at him, blocking out everyone else, especially Dave. "Yes, I do."

Reaching into her shapeless, oversize purse, Kara felt around until she located what she was looking for. Instead of the boxed game she'd brought for Dave, she pulled out a handheld gaming system that had become all but standard issue for every bored kid sitting in the backseat of his or her parents' car, forced to endure yet another cross-country family vacation.

She guessed by the way the little boy's eyes lit up that not only did he not have a copy of the new version—only a few had hit the stores—but he didn't have a handheld set, either.

"Want to play the game?" she offered, holding the gaming system out to him.

"Can I?" he breathed almost reverently. His smile was the closest to beatific she'd ever seen.

She had to restrain herself from hugging the boy. Hugging was something she did when she became emotional. Instead, she nodded and choked out the word "Sure."

"Gary, you'd better not," his mother chided. The woman looked as worn-out as her son. "I don't want to risk having him break it. I can't afford to replace it," she explained.

Her eyes went from the boy to his mother. There was no way she was going to separate Gary from the gaming system. That hadn't been her intent when she'd handed it to him. "I take it he doesn't have one."

Pride entered the woman's face as she squared her shoulders. "We manage just fine."

"I'm sure you do," Kara quickly agreed. "I didn't mean to suggest you didn't." She looked back at the boy. "Would you like to keep that, Gary?"

Gary looked as if he'd suddenly stumbled into paradise. "Can I?" he cried in absolute disbelief.

"No, you can't," his mother told him firmly, even though it clearly hurt her to have to deny him.

Prepared, Kara was quick with her assurances. "It's okay. I work for the company that produces the game. We're giving out a few handheld systems as a way of promoting this latest version."

The boy's mother looked doubtful. Gary looked ecstatic.

"Really?" he cried excitedly, his eyes now bright and as large as proverbial saucers.

Kara had to struggle to contain her own smile. She nodded. "Really."

Gary clutched the system, fully equipped with this newest version of "The Kalico Kid," to his chest. "Thanks, lady!"

Kara solemnly put her hand out to him as if he were a short adult. "My name is Kara—and you're very welcome, Gary."

Gary quickly took her hand and tried to look serious as he shook it, but his grin kept insisting on breaking through.

Kara raised her eyes to look at Gary's mother, half expecting the woman to voice some kind of objection. Instead, she saw tears gathering in the woman's soft brown eyes. Gary's mother mouthed, "Thank you," over the boy's head.

Her mouth curving just a hint, Kara nodded in response.

Behind her, Dave was busy instructing Clarice, telling her to send another one of the patients to the second newly vacated exam room. Done, he turned his attention to Kara.

"I'd like to see you in my office," he told the specter from his childhood.

Kara couldn't help grinning as she followed him around the reception desk, then toward the back of the office. "Bet you've been waiting years to be able to say that line to me."

He bit off his initial response to her flippant remark. After all, she'd just been very kind to one of his regulars. Instead, he waited until Kara had walked into the closet-size office, and then closed the door behind him.

The scarred, faux-mahogany desk listed a little to the right. It and the two chairs, one in front of the desk, one behind it, took up most of the available space. He didn't bother trying to angle his way behind the desk. He anticipated that this was going to be short.

"You're not really having some promotional give-away, are you?" It wasn't a question.

She would have played this out a little longer just to see how far she could take it, but she was running out of time. As senior quality assurance engineer, she was supposed to set an example for the others when it came to keeping decent hours. "No."

"Didn't think so. That was rather a nice thing you just did." He didn't bother going into any details about how very strapped Gary's mother was, or what a brave little person the boy was. That was the kind of stuff that violins were made for and he had a feeling it would be wasted on Kara anyway. It definitely would be on the Kara he remembered.

Or thought he remembered, he amended.

Getting what sounded like a compliment from Dave felt awkward to Kara somehow. Not to mention unsettling. She shrugged, dismissing the words. "Well, I make it a rule not to eat children on Wednesdays."

And then she sobered. Raising her eyes to Dave's green ones, she started to ask, "Does he have—?"

He cut her off, sensing that talking about the disease that had ultimately claimed her father was difficult for her. "It's in remission, but I'm not all that hopeful," he confided.

"That was always your problem," she recalled, not entirely critically. To her, that was just the way things were and she viewed it as something that needed improvement. "Not enough hope, too much practicality."

"You were just the opposite." Almost to the point where she'd stick her head in the ground, he recalled.

She flashed him an irritating smile. "And pleasingly so."

He needed to get back to work before they were literally drowning in patients, and he knew from experience that Kara could keep up the bantering responses all afternoon.

"So, you didn't tell me," he reminded her, taking out his wallet. "How much do I owe you?"

Right, the game. She still hadn't given it to him. Kara dug into her purse again. This time, she pulled out the copy of the video game she'd brought for him. The cellophane around it crinkled as she said, "Your immortal soul."

He pinned her with a look. "Exactly how much is that in cash?"

"I'll let you know." She had no intentions of selling him the game. That made her too much like a lackey. Giving it to him was far better. Besides, she liked the idea of having him indebted to her. "Maybe I'll take it out in trade sometime. I might need something stitched up someday."

He suddenly had an image of her sitting on a rock by the lake, blood running down her leg. The wound had appeared a lot worse than it actually was. That was the summer he'd made up his mind to become a doctor. "You mean like that time at the lake?"

She knew he was referring to that last summer at the lake before he and his family had moved away. She'd been eleven at the time and had slipped on the rocks, trying to elude him after playing some prank. She'd gotten a huge cut on her knee and it wouldn't stop bleeding. She'd valiantly struggled not to cry.

"Those weren't stitches. That was a butterfly bandage you put on it."

The point was that it had done the trick and had held until her father could get her to the emergency room. "Would you have let me come at you with a needle?" he asked.

A rueful smile curved one corner of her mouth. "Point taken, Davy."

He stopped the cringe before it could surface. "No one's called me that in years." She had been the only one to ever do it. Dave looked at her pointedly. "I hate being called Davy."

She grinned, her eyes laughing at him. "I know." She had to get going, and from the sound of the noise in the next room, so did he. "Forget about owing me anything for the game," she told him. "It's on the house. For old times' sake," Kara added.

If she was making restitution for things she'd done to him all those years, this didn't begin to make a dent.

But he saw no point in saying anything. After all, Ryan really wanted the game, and she had been nice to Gary, who had enough hard knocks against him. Besides, saying anything remotely adversarial to Kara would only embroil him in another no-win verbal match. She was probably still a master at that and he wasn't up to one at the moment.

"Thanks." As he said the word, his stomach growled, as if adding a coda.

She stared at him. He couldn't begin to read her expression. Some things never changed, he thought.

"I had no idea you were a ventriloquist."

His stomach growled again, a little softer this time. This was getting embarrassing. "I am on the days I don't get to eat breakfast—or lunch."

She cocked her head, as if she found the information fascinating. "You haven't eaten yet?"

He knew her well enough to wonder what she was up to now. "No."

"But you will."

What kind of a question was that? Everyone had to eat—or expire. "Eventually." He could feel her eyes delving into his skin. Just what did she expect him to say? "Someday," he allowed, then amended his answer to, "Yes," as he brushed past her to get back into the tiny hallway that was desperately in need of a paint job. "Right now there's no time to go get something."

She could see how he couldn't leave, but that didn't mean he had to go hungry. "Why don't you send out Ms. Personality?" When Dave looked at her blankly, she nodded toward the reception room. "The anaconda at the front desk."

MARIE FERRARELLA   33

"We're shorthanded. Clarice's my backup nurse—
and the only one manning the front desk. I can't spare
her, either."

Dave always did make things more complicated
than they were, she recalled. Resigned, she dug into
her purse yet a third time. "In that case, take this."

Though he would have preferred not to admit it,
Dave stared in fascination as the woman from his past
pulled out what appeared to be an entire foot-long sandwich from her purse. It was cut into two equal halves.

What else did she have in there?

"Is that your equivalent to a clown car?" he asked.
"Do you just put your hand in, then pluck an endless
amount of things out?"

She didn't feel like being on the receiving end of
what he might call wit. She had traffic to face and a
game with her name on it waiting to be further decon-
structed. Holding it out to him, she asked, "You want
this roast beef sandwich or not?"

He'd always thought of her as being rather unusual,
but he had a feeling she wasn't given to arbitrarily car-
rying food in her purse. There was only one other explanation for it. "Isn't that your lunch?"

"Well, if you take it, it becomes yours," she pointed
out with a trace of impatience. And then she sighed.
"Look, it's not like I can't buy myself another one on
my way back to the office. You, on the other hand, look
like you haven't a prayer of making it out the door without that gestapo agent throwing a net over you and stopping you before you take three steps."

He felt honor bound to defend the woman working
with him. "Clarice's okay."

"I'm sure. For a gargoyle," Kara agreed. She raised the sandwich a little higher, into his line of vision. "You want this or not?"

She might be annoying, but that was no reason to deprive himself in order to show her he didn't need her help. "I'll take it."

She placed the wax-paper-wrapped sandwich into his hand. "Very kind of you." With that, she turned on her heel to leave.

"Kara?" he called after her.

Pausing, she looked expectantly at Dave over her shoulder. "Yes?"

He still really hadn't thanked her—and found that it was difficult to form the words where she was involved. He settled for: "Tell your mom I said thanks."

Amused, Kara inclined her head and said, "Sure."

That, he knew, was a cop-out on his part. He was better than that, Dave reminded himself. Just because this was Kara shouldn't mean that he reverted back to behaving like an adolescent. "And thanks for bringing it by."

She gave him a quick two-finger salute. "I live to serve."

Same old Kara, same old sarcastic remarks, he thought as he walked out behind her.

"You look good."

The words had slipped out without his permission, going directly from his gut to his tongue without pausing to clear it with his brain. His brain would have definitely vetoed having the words said aloud.

Surprised, Kara stopped abruptly and turned around,

causing a near collision between them. He immediately took a step back.

"Are you addressing that assessment to me in general or just to the back of me?" she asked, an amused smile on her lips.

She could still fluster him, Dave thought. He'd assumed that reaction was years behind him. After all, he'd graduated at the top of his class, been voted into all sorts of positions of honor and had, in general, become confident in not just his abilities but in himself, as well.

Five minutes around Kara and he turned into that gangly, tongue-tied geek whose physique was all but concave the last summer their families had vacationed together.

"Let me think about it," he said evasively.

She nodded. "Thought so."

As she walked out, Gary rose to his feet. "Thank you," he called after her.

She spared the boy a wide smile. This made everything worthwhile. "My pleasure, Gary. All my pleasure."

With that, she was gone.

But not, Dave thought as he turned away to see the patient in room one, forgotten.

Chapter Three

Kara barely had time to run to the sandwich shop to purchase another roast beef sandwich for herself and get back to her desk before her lunch hour was officially over. Just when she'd managed to finally catch her breath, the phone on her desk rang.

Picking it up, she cradled it against her neck and ear. She needed her hands free for the control pad. The newest version of the game still had the pesky Black Knight's horse water surfing.

"Hello?" Kara said absently, guiding the horse and rider over the water to see just how far this glitch extended.

The voice on the other end of the line responded with a single word. "So?"

Kara came to attention as she recognized her mother's voice. The Black Knight and his horse were temporarily forgotten.

"So?" she repeated, having no clue what her mother was asking or saying.

She heard her mother sigh on the other end of the line, then carefully enunciate her question. "Did you bring the game to Dave?"

The question irritated her. Why wouldn't she take the game if she'd already told her mother that she would? "I said I would." She picked up the control pad again. The horse resumed galloping erratically. "Yes, I brought the game to Dave."

"And?"

Kara frowned. Just what was that supposed to mean? "And what?"

A note of frustration entered her mother's voice. "How did he look?"

Damn, the horse just rode off the edge of the earth. This was *not* good. "Like a maniacal serial killer. What do you mean, how did he look? He looked like Dave. Only taller." She paused for a moment, then added, "And handsomer."

"Aha."

"Aha?" Kara repeated, confused. Okay, just where was this conversation headed?

"Never mind," her mother said quickly. "Sorry, I need to go."

Her mother definitely had too much time on her hands. "What you need, Mom, is a hobby." *Other than me,* she added silently. Kara paused to make a notation about the game on the pad she kept by the computer.

"Agreed. Maybe someday you'll give me one," she

thought she heard her mother say. The next moment, the line went dead.

Kara looked thoughtfully at the receiver in her hand. *Maybe someday you'll give me one.* Under ordinary circumstances the most logical "hobby" would be one involving playing on a gaming system. But she had a feeling that her mother was *not* referring to anything as run of the mill as a video game.

And then, just like that, that strange, unsettling feeling that the universe was tilting began to come into focus for her.

The "hobby" her mother was referring to was a grandchild. Her mother wanted a grandchild. And the only way to get one of those, according to her mother, was to get her married and pregnant.

The woman was actually trying to play matchmaker. Damn. Ordinarily, her radar was better than this. How had she missed it?

For the time being, the black stallion was on its own. His aquatic adventures were definitely the last thing on her mind now.

Kara looked at the framed photo on her desk of her mother, her late father and her, taken when she was seventeen. It was the last family photo she had. Looking at her mother now, she shook her head.

"Why, you little sneak. I know what you've been up to. I'm really disappointed in you, Mom," she murmured.

Jake Storm, the man occupying the cubicle next to her, rolled his chair back a little in order to catch a glimpse of her. He had hair and eyebrows that made him look like an affable sheepdog. One shaggy eyebrow arched in amusement now.

"Talking to yourself, Kara?"

She glanced to her right. "No," she told him. "To my mother."

Jake rolled his chair out a little farther, allowing him a clearer view of her space, which was, due to her position in the hierarchy, twice the size of his.

"That would be your invisible mother?" he asked.

"No," she answered. "That would be the meddling mother on the other end of this now defunct phone call." Putting the receiver down, she pushed the offending instrument back on her desk.

"Ah, meddling mothers. Tell me about it. Mine isn't going to be happy until I chuck this game-testing job to the winds, get a degree in something she can brag about, marry the perfect girl and give her three and a half grandchildren—none of which is really doable," he said with a heartfelt sigh, then brightened as he looked at her again. "Unless you're free tonight to drive to Vegas and become Mrs. Jake Storm."

She knew he was kidding. They were friends—without benefits. "And the three and a half kids?" she asked, mildly curious.

"We could rent them." He grinned. "I think a month of endless babysitting might teach my mother a valuable lesson, as in 'careful what you wish for.' Might even be worth the effort," he said wistfully.

However unintentionally, Jake had just given her an idea. A very good idea. She looked at him sharply. "Jake, that's brilliant."

"Clever, maybe," he allowed, "but not brilliant. By

the way—" he leaned in closer "—what clever thing did I just say?"

"Something," Kara told him as she shifted over to the other monitor on her desk, the one directly hooked up to the internet, "that just might get my beloved mother to back off."

"Well, I'm all for that," Jake declared with feeling. Anyone who knew him knew that to be true. His mother was forever trying to set him up with the offspring of her friends. "Let me know how it goes." He nodded toward his own area. "Gotta get back to that crazy horse. He's still walking on water."

"Tell me about it," she murmured under her breath as Jake moved back into his cubicle.

She had no idea what Dave's number was, but she assumed that, as an M.D., he had to be listed *somewhere*. Starting out in the most obvious place, she did a people search through the white pages. The effort took several tries, but ultimately, she came away a winner.

Dialing the phone quickly, she was connected to Dave's office in less than a minute. And then she got to listen to an answering machine. He wasn't in, which only made sense since she'd just seen him at the clinic. His message said his office was closed today.

"Better than nothing," she murmured under her breath with far less enthusiasm than usual as she waited for the outgoing message to end.

If Dave didn't call her back by tonight, she was fairly sure she could find his private number using some creative methods on her laptop at home.

The beep sounded in her ear and she started talking. "Hi, Dave, it's Kara. Remember I said that I'd take that favor out in trade? Well, trading time just arrived. We need to talk. Call me." She rattled off both her cell phone number and the number to her landline in her apartment.

Hanging up, Kara smiled to herself, relishing her plan. Once it got rolling, it would be just what the doctor ordered, she thought, feeling very confident about the outcome. This was going to teach her mother—and possibly Dave's—never to even think about matchmaking again.

Dave was more than a little surprised, when he picked up his messages that evening, to find Kara's among them. Not only was it the only phone message that didn't describe some symptom in depth, but he and she hadn't had any contact in—what, eighteen?—years, and now twice in one day?

Exactly what was up and why did he feel so uneasy about it?

Dropping his mail onto the coffee table, Dave made his way over to the phone on the kitchen wall.

"Only one way to find out," he said aloud. But even so, he didn't begin dialing immediately.

It wasn't that he wanted to renege on the unofficial agreement to reciprocate when she asked. After all, Kara had produced the much sought after game. Then again, how hard could it be for her? She did work for the company that put it out.

Still, she didn't have to deliver it herself—or even give him the game in the first place. Once upon a time, he would have bet his last dime that she wouldn't have given him the time of day, much less gone out of her way, to bring him something he needed.

He also wouldn't have thought that there was a kind bone in her excessively skinny little body. But her treatment of Gary in the waiting room showed him he'd been wrong in his assessment of her. Or at least the "new" her.

No, none of that was holding him back from immediately keeping his word. What *was* stopping him was the hour. He'd just walked in and it was after eleven. Added to that, he was bone tired.

He had no one to blame for that but himself, he thought. Himself and the endless line of sick people who just kept on coming. Clarice had finally closed the doors two hours later than the clinic's official closing time. And he'd gone on treating patients until there was no one left in the stale-smelling waiting room.

Now, two steps beyond dead tired, he was too exhausted to even get anything to eat out of the refrigerator. One way to lose weight, he mused. That sandwich Kara had pulled out of her magic bag was practically the only solid thing he had to eat all day until Clarice had called her grandson to bring some food from the Thai takeout place in her neighborhood. He hadn't really recognized what he'd eaten, but whatever it was had substance to it and ultimately had helped to keep him going, which was what counted.

His mind came back full circle to Kara. Okay, she'd given him a game and her sandwich. If nothing else, that meant he needed to return her phone call.

And if, God willing, she didn't answer, well, at least he was on record for trying. Recorded record. He punched out her numbers on the keypad and crossed his fingers that she didn't answer, but he might as well have saved himself the trouble. Kara picked up her phone on the second ring.

"Hello?"

Her voice sounded a bit sleepy, he thought. An image of Kara in bed, wearing nothing but the moonlight breaking through her window, suddenly popped up in his head.

He really needed that social life he was sorely missing out on.

"Hello?" he heard her say again.

He dove in. "Kara, it's Dave. You called."

At the sound of his voice, Kara dragged herself up into a sitting position. She'd fallen asleep on her sofa, playing a portable version of the game that was bedeviling her and the staff she supervised. She struggled to clear the fog from her brain. She didn't even remember shutting her eyes.

Squinting, she tried to make out the time on the cable box across the room. The numbers swam around, and she gave up.

"Right. I called," she murmured, dragging her hand through her hair, trying to figuratively drag her thoughts together at the same time.

"About anything in particular?" Dave pressed. She sounded sluggish. He thought back and couldn't remember a time when she wasn't going ninety miles an hour. "Because if this can wait, or you just called to yank my chain, it's been a really long day and I've got an early call tomorrow in the hospital—"

She wasn't about to give him a chance to hang up.

From the sound of it, she was going to have to make an appointment to talk to him on the phone if she didn't speak up quickly. So she did. "Our mothers are trying to set us up."

"What? With who?" he asked incredulously.

Was he kidding? "What do you mean, with who? With each other. At least," she amended, backtracking just a step, "I know mine is, and whatever mine does, yours usually does, too."

When did this happen? It wasn't making any sense. She must have made a mistake. "What are you talking about?" he demanded.

She took a breath and explained how she'd come to this conclusion. "After I came back from your clinic, my mother called me at work to see if I'd given you the game."

"She obviously knows how dependable you are," he observed dryly.

Her back instantly went up. "I'll have you know that I am— Never mind."

This wasn't the time to allow herself to get into an argument with him. They were both tired. Things could be said that couldn't be retracted. The best way to prevent that was not to start anything at all. Besides, she had a far more important point to get to. She couldn't allow herself to get sidetracked.

"Anyway, she wanted to know how you looked. More accurately, she wanted to know what *I* thought of the way you looked."

So far, he wasn't hearing anything that should have set off any whirling red lights for her. "Natural question," he commented. "We haven't seen each other in almost two decades."

She stopped her narrative, struggling with her temper. Was he for real? Or was he just baiting her? If it was the latter, maybe he'd learned a thing or two since they'd last seen each other. But somehow, she doubted that. He'd always been too upstanding to stoop to anything.

"Were you always this naive, or did you just suddenly decide to go back to your childhood?"

He really wasn't in the mood for this. "If you're going to insult me—"

"Tempting, but I'll save that for some other time. Right now, hard as it is for me, I need to ask you for your help."

Dave interpreted her question the only way he knew how. "You have a medical question?"

"No, I have a mother question. Or rather, a solution to a meddling-mother situation." He was very quiet on the other end. Was that a good sign, or had he fallen asleep? "Our mothers want to get us together. I never told you," she segued quickly, "but I once overheard them talking about how terrific it would be if, when you and I grew up, we'd get married."

His voice was stripped of all emotion as he said, "No, you never told me that."

"At the time I heard it, I thought it was too gross to repeat," she explained. "But it obviously has never stopped being on their minds."

He was trying to follow her logic and found that there were gaping holes in it. "And you think that your mother calling you to see if you delivered the game to me is actually some kind of a confession on her part that she's trying to get us to the altar?"

She knew he was mocking her and forced herself to swallow a few choice words. "Her asking me what I think of your looks is pretty transparent."

Where was all this going, anyway? "So you called to warn me?"

She shifted the phone to her other ear. "No, I called to get you to cooperate with an idea I have."

He *really* didn't like the sound of that. "This never turned out well for any of the characters in those sit-coms you always liked so much," Dave pointed out.

That he remembered she used to watch them aston-ished her. She told herself it meant nothing and kept talking. "What if you and I pretend to go out together? Pretend to, you know, like each other."

It sounded as if she were forcing herself to endure a fate worse than death. "Assuming I've had my rabies shots," he said sarcastically, "how is this going to teach our mothers a lesson? This is what they want— according to you."

Kara sighed. "You really don't have an imagination, do you?"

"I have one," he told her. "I just don't let it go off on wild tangents."

She took offense and shot back through gritted teeth, "Okay, *Davy,* let me spell it out for you. We go out. We pretend to fall in love, and then we have one hell of an argument, making sure that we have this fight where our mothers can hear us. After the argument, we go through the throes of an agonizing 'breakup.' A dev-astating breakup," she specified, really throwing herself into the role, "where we both act as if there's no tomorrow—"

"Being just a little melodramatic, don't you think?" he interjected.

He really was spoiling for a fight, wasn't he? Not that she was intimidated, but she wanted this to get under way quickly. The sooner the better.

"Maybe. We'll have to play it by ear. But they'll be so upset that we're upset, I guarantee that it'll cure them once and for all from trying to play matchmaker with us on any level—separately or together." She paused to take a breath. "What do you think? You game?"

If he said no, he had a feeling she'd keep calling and badgering him until he agreed. Still, throwing his lot in with Kara made him uneasy.

"Why do I get the feeling that I'm about to sign my own death warrant?"

What was it about him that set her off like this? Eighteen years and nothing had changed. Except that he was better looking, but that had no bearing here.

"Because you're running on next to no sleep, you have no imagination and you don't know a good plan when you hear one. Shall I go on?"

He laughed shortly. "Not that I have the slightest doubt that you could, but please don't."

She was still waiting for an answer. "Does that mean no?"

This was the moment of truth. He could still walk away. But he had a feeling that she had a point. Though he loved his mother dearly, he could think of nothing he wanted less than to have her playing matchmaker on his behalf.

"That means that I'm probably going to really regret this, but you do have a point."

Yes! "Glad you recognize that."

He wanted to move this along while he still had a prayer of getting some sleep. "All right, mastermind, so what's our next move?" he asked her.

She would have thought that was self-evident. "We pretend to go out."

"And what, notify the press first? How are our mothers going to know we're going out? I think they'd be suspicious if either one of us just picked up the phone and called to tell them."

She smiled. He was almost cute when he tried to be flippant. The key word here was *almost*.

"Ah, there is more than just space between those manly ears. You're absolutely right. How about that birthday for your cousin's son?" she asked. "The one I got you the video game for."

"Ryan," he supplied.

"Ryan," she repeated. "Ryan's going to have a birthday party, right?"

"Yes—" He got no further.

Kara pounced on the next question. "Is your mother going to be there?"

Okay, so now it was all crystal clear to him. Not bad, he acknowledged, albeit silently. Saying it out loud would just give her a bigger head. "Yes."

"Okay, then we will be, too. All we need is one eye-witnessing mother to spread the news to the other."

"Eyewitnessing," he echoed. "Is that even a word?"

"It is for this purpose," she said glibly. "Anyway,

they'll think their plan is working—until we show them otherwise. So, are you in?"

"I'm in," he answered even as part of him had the sinking feeling that by agreeing, life as he knew it would never be the same again. This very well could be a huge mistake.

Joining forces with Kara was always dangerous. It was a known fact that she possessed a golden tongue. It was also a known fact that she could abruptly leave him holding the bag if it suited her purposes.

He had no reason to believe that eighteen years had changed anything, her greatly improved figure notwithstanding.

Chapter Four

The phone rang just as Paulette walked past it. On her way out, she debated just letting the answering machine pick it up. But there was something about a ringing phone that always captured her attention to the exclusion of everything else. It was irresistible.

Pausing, she lifted the receiver from the cradle and brought it to her ear. "Hello?"

"I thought you'd want to be the first to know—well, not really first, but close," the voice on the other end said.

Lisa. Paulette dropped her purse to the floor, kicked off the high heels she'd just slipped on and deposited her body into the overstuffed chair in her living room. There was no such thing as a quick exchange of words between her and Lisa.

"Almost the first to know what?" Paulette asked.

Even as she did so, she mentally crossed her fingers, hoping that her little plan had succeeded in its next stage.

"That Dave called Melissa and asked her if she'd mind if he brought someone to Ryan's birthday party."

Paulette could hear the smile in her friend's voice. It mirrored the one on her own face. "And this friend wouldn't be Kara, by any chance, would it?"

At this point, it was a rhetorical question. She sincerely doubted that Lisa would be calling her to say that her son was bringing someone else to the little boy's party.

And then Lisa confirmed all her hopes by saying, "Yes, it would."

Paulette would have clapped her hands together with glee if both of them had been free. "See, I told you so. All it took was for the two of them to be in the same place at the same time." And just like that, she was flying high on confidence. "The rest will soon be history."

"Don't start sending out the wedding invitations just yet," Lisa cautioned. "I mean, it's not like Dave hasn't dated before. And you've told me that Kara has gone out with a few guys from time to time. Wasn't there that guy, Alex something-or-other, she was seeing pretty regularly a while back?"

The name instantly brought a wave of anger. "You mean the bigamist?"

"He was *married?*" Lisa asked, horrified.

"Well, not exactly," Paulette backtracked. "But he *was* seeing several women at the same time, including a live-in girlfriend who just *happened* to be the mother of his little boy. Kara was devastated when she accidentally found out—devastated and furious. He's the one who made her swear off having anything to do with men."

At the time that it happened, she'd kept the news to herself in deference to Kara's wishes. But in her opinion enough time had passed for the truth to finally come out. Besides, she wanted Lisa to know that her daughter wasn't a wallflower because no one was interested. She was one by choice.

"I don't think you realize what this actually means," Paulette continued.

"Enlighten me," Lisa urged.

"If Kara actually agreed to go out with Dave, it means she's ready to get back into life. This is a really big deal," Paulette enthused. "Why don't we get together at the end of this week and celebrate?"

As ever, Paulette was getting ahead of herself, Lisa thought. "A family gathering for a child's birthday doesn't exactly fall into the same parameters as a date," Lisa pointed out.

"Walking down the block holding hands is a date," Paulette insisted. "Anything involving two consenting people is considered a *date*. C'mon, Lis, don't rain on my parade."

It wasn't that she wasn't as hopeful about the outcome of all this as Paulette was, it was just that she was a little more grounded than her friend. And yes, a little more pessimistic.

"I'm not raining on it, Paulette, I just want you to have an umbrella handy—just in case," Lisa explained.

"By the way, about Ryan's party… There's always room for one more. Would you like to come?"

"You know I would, but…"

Lisa thought that Paulette would have jumped at the chance to be there to watch over her daughter interacting with Dave. "But?" she questioned.

"If I'm there, Kara might feel self-conscious and not be herself." Her daughter also might think she was being spied on, Paulette thought.

Lisa sighed, considering Paulette's reasoning. "I suppose you have a point."

Paulette paused, chewing on her lower lip. "On the other hand, I also have an insatiable desire to see them finally come together." She weighed the two sides for a moment, thinking. Desire won out over sensibility. "Oh, what the hell? Count me in."

Lisa laughed. As if there was ever any real doubt, she thought. "Consider it done. I'll call Melissa right now," she said, ending their phone call.

This was taking way too long. By all rights, it should have been a snap, Kara told herself as she took yet another outfit out of her closet and looked it over carefully.

Ordinarily, she'd reach into her closet and throw just about anything on. Or, at the very least, she wouldn't regard everything she'd taken out with such a critical eye.

Why did how she looked matter so much? She upbraided herself.

The problem was that she worked for a company that had no dress code—beyond requiring that their employees show up at work clothed. During the summer she went in wearing a tank top and shorts half the time. And since she hadn't had a date since the Alex fiasco had burned her so badly, all of the things she might normally wear for any sort of actual occasion had been pushed to the back of her closet. Now, as she pulled them out, she kept finding something wrong with each outfit.

What was the matter with her? This was just Davy she was going with. Comfortable, old stick-in-the-mud Davy. And this was all pretend, anyway. There was no need to fuss like this.

"Damn it," she said to her reflection in the wardrobe mirror. "It's a kid's party. A stained T-shirt and dirty jeans would probably blend right in."

Even so, she took out yet another garment, this time a light blue sundress with white piping along the edges of the skirt, spaghetti straps and bodice. Holding it up against herself, she decided that it was as good as anything she'd pulled out so far. Maybe a tad better than most. For one thing, the color brought out her eyes and the dress's waistline brought out her own.

Finally.

Or maybe—

Kara glanced at her watch. How had it gotten to be so late? This was supposed to take her only ten minutes, not an hour. The party was beginning in less than half an hour.

"Sundress, it is," she declared.

She'd no sooner shed her tank top and shorts and put the sundress on than her doorbell rang.

Now what? she wondered. She wasn't expecting anyone.

Maybe it was the new gaming system she'd ordered, Kara thought hopefully. It wasn't scheduled to be delivered until next week, but you never knew. Once in a blue moon the mail actually arrived before it was supposed to.

Leaving the dress unzipped in the back—she wasn't planning on walking away from the mailman—Kara hurried to the door.

"Coming!" she called out, hoping the mail carrier wouldn't leave before she got there.

She yanked the door open, and disappointment descended swiftly. "You're not the mail carrier."

"Very observant," Dave commented. "Were you expecting him?"

"Well, I wasn't expecting you," she informed him crisply.

Since she wasn't inviting him in, Dave took hold of her shoulders, moved her slightly to one side and walked into the apartment on his own.

"Correct me if I'm wrong, but weren't you the one who said we're supposed to be 'pretending' to be on a date while attending Ryan's birthday party?"

God, but he irritated her, she thought. There was no reason to talk down to her like this. "Yes, but I thought we were meeting there—at Melissa's house."

"It occurred to me while driving to the party that arriving in separate cars didn't seem very datelike," he pointed out. "Is that how all your dates go? Because if so, I might have the answer as to why you're still unattached."

Maybe she should just kill him here now and be done with it. The idea had definite appeal.

"You could have called and given me a warning. And never mind how my dates go," Kara snapped, closing the door he'd left open. She frowned, then shrugged. "Well, since you're here, I guess we can go to the birthday party together. But I'm not ready yet," she informed him. When he raised a quizzical eyebrow she explained, "I don't have my shoes on."

"I thought you looked shorter." And then his mouth curved in a half-amused smile as she moved away. "You don't exactly have your dress on yet, either."

She turned back and looked at him sharply. "What are you talking about?" she demanded.

Rather than answer her, he turned her around and then zipped up her dress, his knuckles lightly skimming along her bare skin.

Something warm and shivery shimmied up and down her spine, discharging tiny zaps of electricity as it went. Kara struggled not to let the tingling sensation get to her.

"There," Dave pronounced. "You're decent. It's a kid's party. Ryan's precocious for his age, but he's a little too young to see his first half-naked woman, no matter how tempting the sight might be."

Her temper flared. "I'm not—" The rest of his statement suddenly hit. "Wait, did you say 'tempting'?"

That had been a careless slip on his part. He had to remember that Kara pounced on the least little thing. "Just a general observation," he said mildly. Shoving his hands into the pockets of his slacks, he deliberately moved away from her and looked around the room.

"Nice place," he commented. "A little claustrophobic for my taste, but nice."

She'd forgotten about that. Dave had been claustrophobic as a kid. The second she'd found out, she'd taken every opportunity to put him to the test. She herself was fearless and couldn't fathom anyone breaking into a sweat just because they were confined to a tiny little space.

"Thanks," Kara responded.

Preoccupied, she was still mulling over his "tempting" remark. Had that been a slip of the tongue or just a word he'd used carelessly? There was nothing in his tone or his facial expression that gave her the slightest clue.

Most likely, she decided, he was setting up a joke at her expense. There was no reason to believe just because he'd become a doctor who volunteered at a free clinic once a week that he'd suddenly become a noble specimen of manhood. At least, not as far as she was concerned, anyway.

Getting her shoes, Kara stepped into them and then grabbed her purse from the coffee table before pausing to pick up a large shopping bag next to the sofa.

With a toss of her head, she announced, "Okay, I'm ready."

Dave began to walk out. Noticing the shopping bag, he nodded at it. "What's that?"

"A present for Ryan. You didn't expect me to go to this party empty-handed, did you?"

When it came to Kara, he really didn't know what to expect. He never had. The logic he cherished had no place in her life.

"I thought 'The Kalico Kid' game was from both of us," he admitted. "Reinforces this dating thing you're trying to sell everyone on."

"Not *everyone*," she corrected. "Just our mothers, remember? And as far as *reinforcing* anything, coming with one video game between the two of us only reinforces the idea that we're cheap since I do work for a video game company."

"Ryan doesn't know that," he pointed out. "And I suggest that if you don't want to find yourself under attack from a whole bunch of kids, you might think twice before making that little fact public knowledge at the party."

She looked at him in silence for a moment, then smiled. "If I didn't know better, Davy, I'd say you were being thoughtful."

"I was being practical," he corrected. "And I've asked you before, don't call me Davy," he added with feeling.

They walked out the door, and he waited until she locked up, then led the way to his car. "So what are you giving him?"

The company was releasing two new games at the beginning of the month. Senior engineers were allowed to get the first copies. She was passing hers on to Ryan but she didn't want to say as much to Dave, so all she said was, "You'll see."

When they came to a stop before a gleaming red sports car in the guest parking, she looked at him incredulously. This did *not* go with his usual image. "This isn't your car, is it?"

He might have known she'd have some kind of crack

about it. Admittedly, it was an indulgence. He'd just gotten rid of the secondhand car he'd been driving since his senior year of college. Since it had been so reliable, he hadn't wanted to give it up until it wasn't functioning anymore.

Dave braced himself for a punch line. "Why wouldn't this be mine?"

"Because it's sleek and powerful with a hell of a lot of horsepower." *And a damn beautiful vehicle,* she added silently, then raised her eyes to his. "Everything you're supposedly not."

"You have no idea what I am, Kara," he informed her coolly. Hitting the security release on his keychain, he unlocked the car doors, then nodded toward the passenger side. "Get in."

Kara opened the car door and looked inside. There was still the faint new-car smell. The interior was utterly pristine. No junk, no crumbs, not a single thing to testify that anyone had even ridden in the car. Her own car looked as if she were living out of it. She was glad he hadn't seen it. It would only give him added ammunition to make fun of her.

Getting in and buckling her seat belt, she said, "You just had this detailed, didn't you?"

"Detailed?" he repeated as he did the same, his eyebrows drawing together over a nose that would make sculptors and plastic surgeons alike weak with envy. "What do you mean by 'detailed'?"

He watched as a smile unfurled on her lips. If it hadn't been at his expense, he would have enjoyed the sight.

"I forgot. You're not a car person."

"I think the word you're looking for is *fanatic*. Car *fanatic*," he said pointedly.

She knew he was just saying that because he felt lacking in that department—and embarrassed about it. She doubted if the E.R. doctor knew very much beyond where the key went and where he put the gas. Still, she couldn't help bristling at the put-down.

"There's nothing fanatical about knowing how a car works or where the dipstick goes," she informed him haughtily.

"I have a suggestion where to put the dipstick," he muttered under his breath. "And if you really want to convince anyone that I'd actually voluntarily spend time with you, I suggest you stop being so damn antagonistic and taking apart everything I say."

Instantly, Kara felt her back go up. "I don't—"

She got no further. Inserting the key into the ignition, Dave gave her a look that said, "Yes, you do." The awful part was that she knew she really couldn't argue with him. She was being antagonistic, but only because she felt he was being condescending.

The reason didn't matter, she told herself. She had to work on her attitude, work on her delivery. Neither of their mothers were going to be taken in by this charade if they saw her with her hands wrapped around Dave's throat, choking the life out of him.

She paused to pull herself together before saying anything. Two deep breaths later, she finally murmured, "Sorry." Another fortifying deep breath came and went before she added, "I'll try to act like I think you're the greatest thing since sliced bread."

"Don't go overboard," he cautioned. "Neither of our

mothers is going to buy into that. If you ask me, they're not even going to buy that we're dating."

He was wrong there and she really wanted to say it that way, but she settled for a more diplomatic delivery. "They'll buy into it because that's what they were hoping for by sending me to you bearing a video game, remember?" She thought for a moment, searching for a plausible excuse as to why they initially got together. "We can tell them, if they ask why we're seeing each other, that we're catching up on the years since we last saw each other. Since that covers about eighteen years, it should take us a bit."

"Sounds reasonable enough, I guess," he conceded. "But to make that work, you realize we're actually going to have to exchange some information."

He sounded as if he was putting her on notice, she thought. She had nothing to hide. Her only problem was going to be staying awake to listen to eighteen years of his life.

"I'm game," she told him.

Dave pressed down on the accelerator, making it through the light at the crosswalk just before it turned red.

"Okay, what have you been doing these last eighteen years—in fifty words or less?" he qualified as she opened her mouth.

This, Kara thought darkly, was definitely not going to be a walk in the park. Why in heaven's name would her mother think she would *ever* want to become romantically involved with this man? Other than his looks and maybe his selflessness, he had nothing going for him.

She reminded herself that this was to teach her mother a lesson. Eventually, it would all be worth it. If she survived.

Chapter Five

"I take it your cousin likes balloons," Kara observed, an amused smile curving her lips.

There'd been three balloons, one blue, one white, one yellow, attached to the sign right outside his cousin's residential development along with an arrow pointing the way to the party. Another three balloons, comprised of the same colors, and another arrow were on the street sign at the first corner. Three more balloons again at the next turn and so on until they had reached the block—a cul-de-sac—where the party was taking place and, if parked cars and noise level were any indication, was currently in full swing.

She could see that the mailbox of a two-story house in the center of the block had not just three but six balloons, again comprised of the same three colors, indicating journey's end. As if that were actually necessary.

"Melissa just didn't want to take the chance that anyone would go the wrong way," Dave told her as they entered the cul-de-sac.

He pulled up into the first available parking space he saw. It was also the *last* available parking space on either side of the street. A convention of SUVs hugged every available inch of curb space not only along both sides of the block, but trickling down toward the next block, as well.

Dave unbuckled his seat belt. But as he started to get out, Kara put her hand on his wrist, stopping him. Puzzled, he looked at her. "Change your mind?"

Having gotten him to play along, there was no way she was going to abandon her plan now. That was the whole point.

"No, I just want to remind you that we're supposed to be into each other. That means you're going to have to hold my hand and not look at me as if you'd really rather be attending my vivisection."

He deliberately looked intrigued. "You're having a vivisection?"

"Don't get cute. You know what I mean. Just act as if you actually like me."

He shook his head, a dubious expression on his face. "That's an awful lot of acting you're asking for," he cracked. "I don't know if I'm up to it.

Her eyes held his, trying to determine if he was being flippant or if there was more than a small vein of truth to his words. Maybe it was time to have it out in the open.

"You hate me that much?" she wanted to know.

He thought he heard a hint of vulnerability in her

voice. Probably just his imagination. He really doubted that Kara had had a vulnerable moment in her life. But on the outside chance that her question was actually serious—and that his answer mattered—he told her the truth.

"I never hated you—well, almost never," he amended, remembering a couple of incidents that involved purple paint and a great many showers afterward. He'd lost count just how many it had taken to get the hue off his skin the second time. "It was more that I was very leery of you. I never knew what you were going to pull next."

Okay, maybe she had been a little hard on him, but it wasn't as if he was an innocent in all this. "Maybe if you hadn't treated me like I was contagious, stupid and beneath you, I wouldn't have pulled anything." He looked at her for a long moment without saying a word. But she could read his expression. "Okay," she relented, amending her initial statement. "Maybe a few things, but you would have never had to submit yourself to being scrubbed down with nail polish remover."

He'd forgotten about that. The distance of time allowed him to laugh at the memory. "I guess I should count myself lucky that I even survived my childhood with you around."

"That goes double for me," she countered.

He looked at her incredulously. Was she kidding? Or did she think he had amnesia? There were times she'd made his life a living hell.

"You? Ha!"

"What do you mean, 'ha'?" she challenged, ready to

66   *THE LAST FIRST KISS*

go a few rounds with him right now, the party and her
mother notwithstanding.

"You were Kara Calhoun. You were invincible. As
invincible," he recalled, "as the comic-book heroine
your dad named you after."

He'd thought that? Somehow, she found it difficult
to believe. But then, if he didn't believe it, why had he
just said it? Agreeing to her fallibility would have been
more in keeping with his regular behavior, at least as it
applied to her.

Something to puzzle over later, Kara told herself.
Right now, they had mothers to fool.

"All water under the bridge," she said with a shrug,
getting out of his car.

Rising, he closed the door on his side. "Gee, that's a
clever saying. Mind if I use it sometime?"

"And we're back," she commented. But rather than
being cryptic, she coupled the comment with a grin that
she flashed at him.

A grin, Dave thought, that was oddly and perversely
appealing. Which only meant that he needed to get in
out of the sun before his brain was completely fried,
he decided as he rounded the back of his vehicle and
stepped onto the sidewalk next to Kara.

"All right, let's get this over with." Then, pausing
to brace himself—an exaggerated moment for her
benefit—he took Kara's hand in his.

She leaned her head slightly into his and whispered, "It'd be a bit more romantic if your teeth weren't
clenched."

"Baby steps, Kara. Baby steps," he replied as he
walked toward the house.

Kara did her best not to notice that when his hand enveloped hers, a strange feeling of well-being, of protection, washed over her. It was almost as if something inside her felt that all was well in heaven and God was in His kingdom.

She would have philosophically chalked it up to pre-performance jitters, except that she'd never had any, not even when she'd taken to the actual stage in elementary school. She was a ham and loved the spotlight, loved being the focus of attention. This, however, felt different somehow. She decided now wasn't the time to explore why.

"Showtime," she murmured to Dave as they stood on the front porch, which was completely festooned with balloons.

Dave said nothing as he rang the doorbell. A moment later, the door opened. Dave's cousin Melissa was a tall, willowy, dark-haired woman with an easy, welcoming smile. A smile, Kara realized, that resembled Dave's a great deal.

Not that it mattered.

"Kara," she greeted her warmly. "Dave said he'd be bringing you." Taking Kara's free hand in both of hers, Melissa lowered her voice before continuing, "I can't thank you enough for getting that game for Ryan. He's talked about nothing else since he saw the first commercial for it two months ago. Every place I tried was sold out and told me they would be for weeks. My husband, Simon, and I really hated knowing he was going to be disappointed, but now because of you, he isn't going to be." Dave's cousin underscored her statement by giving Kara a fierce hug.

She was surprised that Dave had actually given her credit in this matter. Maybe he wasn't as easy to read as she'd initially thought.

Released from the bear hug, Kara brushed off the woman's thanks quickly. "Part of the perks for working at a company that pays dirt," she confided flippantly. "I brought Ryan a few other games," she added, raising the shopping bag in her hand. "They're all age-appropriate," she assured Melissa.

"I may never get Ryan to go to bed again." Melissa laughed. "Just leave it on the birthday pile over there." She pointed out a card table that had been set up on the side. Someone was calling her name and she was already withdrawing. "There are beverages in the kitchen and snacks all over the place. Please help yourself to anything you want."

Pointedly, if perhaps a beat belatedly, Kara looked at Dave and told his cousin, "I already have everything I want."

She hoped it wasn't obvious that the words had stuck in her throat and had to be forced out. Dave, to his credit, didn't look surprised. He remembered the plan. When she slanted a glance toward his cousin, Melissa was beaming, as if she was genuinely thrilled for them.

Obviously everyone in his family had, until now, just assumed Dave was going to remain a grumpy, unattached bachelor for the rest of his life, Kara thought. Apparently she was regarded as the answer to their prayers.

"Your mom's already here," Melissa told Dave, then glanced back at Kara. "Yours, too."

Kara stretched her lips back in a smile that Dave

found unreadable—but he could make an educated guess as to the feeling behind it.

"Wonderful," Kara commented. Looking at Dave, she said, "Let's put the gifts on the table, Dave." At the last minute, she stopped herself from adding the *y*, managing to stretch out his name instead.

"Sure, Kara."

"Try not to sound so stilted," she whispered as they walked away, taking care that Melissa didn't overhear them.

"That's my everyday voice," he told her, irritated. Was there anything she didn't feel compelled to edit?

"I know."

Dave let out a long breath but said nothing.

Leading the way to the growing pile of birthday gifts, Kara took the games she'd wrapped less than an hour ago and deposited them on top. Dave waited until she was finished, then added his to the stack.

"Laying it on a little thick back there, weren't you?" he asked her.

"Melissa obviously didn't think so," Kara pointed out. "She looked happy."

If that made her feel guilty, she was determined not to dwell on it. The old saying about breaking eggs and making omelets echoed in her brain.

"Besides," she continued, also keeping her voice low, "the more in love everyone thinks we are, the more impact the breakup will have. My mother—and yours—will feel just awful that their misguided matchmaking efforts brought us nothing but pain. In the end, that should keep them from ever attempting anything like this again. I figure that's a good thing—unless you actually like being set up on blind dates."

Dave shivered at the mere suggestion of it. "God, no."

"Okay, then we're agreed." She looked around but didn't see her mother or his. Maybe their "audience" was out back with the children, she thought. "Could you get me something to drink?" she said to Dave.

Instead of doing as she asked, Dave physically turned her toward the kitchen and pointed. "Kitchen's right through there. You can get it yourself."

That wasn't the point. No wonder he was still unattached, she thought. "You're supposed to be willing to slay dragons for me," she told him. "You can't get a simple can of soda?"

"I'm saving my strength for the dragons," he answered. "Besides, I figured you'd be insulted if I usurped your right to choose your own beverage. Trampling on your independence and all that sort of thing," he elaborated when she looked at him quizzically.

Did he think she was that neurotic and insecure? "My independence is alive and well, thank you." Well, they were supposed to be inseparable at this stage in their relationship, she thought. At least, so she'd heard. "Tell you what," she proposed, taking his hand and lacing her fingers through his, "we'll both go. I mean, since we're in the beginning stages of euphoric infatuation. It only stands to reason that we'd want to spend every minute we can together, right?"

He looked at her, a little stunned. "You really plotted all this out, didn't you?"

Kara raised her eyebrows until they disappeared beneath her feathery bangs. "And this surprises you?"

He thought back to all the elaborate tricks she'd played on him those summers he was forced to endure her company. Now that he reexamined them, a lot of planning must have gone into those tricks. She'd been a mini-Napoleon. Obviously, she still was.

"No, not really," he conceded. And then a thought struck him. "This isn't going to involve one of us getting left at the altar, is it?" Because if it did, he had a sinking feeling it would be him. He saw no reason for him to have to endure any sort of humiliation in this little charade of hers.

She stopped abruptly and looked at him. She hadn't thought of that before. "No, but that's not a bad idea," she said as she turned it over in her head.

"Yes, it is," he contradicted firmly. "A very bad idea."

"Okay, I'll shelve it," she said agreeably as she resumed walking. "Temporarily." She sidestepped another couple, flashing an absent smile at them even though she had no idea who they were.

Dave nodded at the couple. "You'll shelve it permanently," he snarled between clenched teeth, "or this stops right here."

"Down, boy," she soothed, placing a calming hand on his chest—which only irritated him further. "We're not up to the part where we have public tiffs yet." He made no response but his glare was boring a hole right through her. "Okay, you win," she surrendered. "No getting left at the altar." Kara cocked her head, giving it one last try. "Not even if it's me?"

Dave's one-word answer came quickly and firmly. "No."

She thought that her being the one would have changed everything in his eyes. She was convinced the man would have enjoyed having a front-row seat to her humiliation, especially if it was in public. "Just curious. Why?"

"Because bailing out at the last minute and leaving you standing alone at the altar just isn't something I'd do, and everyone knows it." Because there were people within earshot, he lowered his head and his voice, talking into her ear. "Besides, that would put people in a really awkward position—not to mention there's also the expense of getting a sitter for the afternoon, buying a wedding gift, maybe buying new clothes for the occasion, all for ultimately no reason." There was more but he stopped abruptly because she was staring at him in amazement. "What?" he demanded.

It was a struggle for her to ignore the effect of his warm breath along not just her neck but other parts of her body, as well. Instead, she forced herself to focus on what he'd just said. "I forgot how you could over-think things."

"The other side of that is that you *under*-think them," he pointed out.

"There's no such word," she pointed out, the wide smile on her lips for everyone else's benefit so that the people at the party would think they were just indulging in lovers' talk.

Dave snorted. "Maybe not, but in your world, there should be."

Reaching the kitchen, she crossed to the refrigerator

and opened it. The beverages she was interested in—diet soda—were lined up on the bottom shelf. She bent over to look at the various labels.

"What's your pleasure?" she asked, turning around various cans and bottles to examine their names.

Dave watched, almost against his will, as the back of the narrow skirt of her sundress hiked up to a new, mesmerizing height, stopping just at the tops of the back of her thighs and managing to tantalize him.

You.

The word flashed through his mind in response to her question, surprising him probably more than it would her had he said it out loud.

Dave smothered both the word and the feeling as quickly as if it were a sudden spark in a tinder-dry forest.

Hearing no answer, Kara, still bent over the shelf, looked at him over her shoulder. "Dave?" she prodded.

"Anything," he said quickly, looking away as if someone had called to him. "I don't care."

"Okay." Taking a can of a popular brand of diet cola in each hand, she stood up, turned around and handed one to him. "Anything, it is."

The paper cups were on the counter directly behind Dave, and Kara brushed against him as she reached for one for herself. The unexpected jolt of electricity that raced through him had him convinced that this, coming here with her, was a bad idea. Definitely a very bad idea.

Served him right for listening to her, he upbraided himself.

As he heard several people enter the room, he saw

Kara tense ever so slightly. He didn't have to turn around to know why, but he did anyway. Just in time to see Kara's mother crossing to them. Or perhaps it was the refrigerator that was the object of her focus.

Rather than greet her daughter, the petite woman turned her attention and remarkable blue eyes exclusively on him. The smile on her lips lit up her whole face, and her eyes crinkled as she took his hand and shook it.

"Dave," she cried warmly. "It's so nice to see you again. Your mother's been telling me all good things about you."

He knew how much his mother liked to brag about him. Though he loved her dearly, it made him uncomfortable. Dave shrugged in response. "She likes to exaggerate."

"Oh, I doubt that, Dave," Paulette assured him, still not looking at Kara. "I've known your mother a very long time. Exaggeration isn't in her nature. Why, thank you," she said as he handed her the can of soda Kara had just given him a moment earlier. Briefly, her eyes shifted toward Kara, then back to him. Popping the top of the can, she picked up a paper cup and filled it halfway before asking, "Who's your friend?"

This, Kara knew, was a not-too-veiled comment on the fact that, according to her mother, they didn't see each other nearly enough. Working overtime at the company meant she had enough time to go to and from work, then crash as she tried to eat a very late dinner. It left no time for visiting.

"Very funny, Mom."

"Mom," Paulette repeated as if she were tasting the

word for flavor and then turning it over in her mind. "I seem to remember knowing someone who used to call me that," she told Dave. "But for the life of me, I can't seem to recall who. I just have this vague feeling that I haven't seen that person in ages."

"And you might not," Kara warned, "if you keep this up. And you—" she turned toward Dave "—stop smirking. It's only encouraging her, and God knows she doesn't need any encouragement."

Paulette patted Dave's arm and offered him a very conspiratorial smile. "Her bark has always been worse than her bite, Dave," she assured him. "Kara might seem rather prickly, but on the inside, she's really a softie. You just have to be patient. Sometimes it takes longer to surface."

He doubted if there was that much patience in the world, but he kept that to himself. Instead, he said dutifully, "Yes, ma'am."

Paulette smiled. It was obvious that she was allowing herself a moment to dream. And by her expression, Kara had a sneaking suspicion she knew exactly what her mother was dreaming.

Not in a million years, Mom. Sorry.

"I always liked you, Dave," Paulette told him with feeling. She sifted her eyes toward her daughter. The smile cooled a little. "You, I'm not so sure about." Picking up both the paper cup and the can of soda, her eyes swept over both of them. "Carry on, you two," she urged as she left the room. "And I mean that from the bottom of my heart."

Kara rolled her eyes, refusing to look in Dave's direction. There had been train wrecks that were subtler than her mother, she thought in dismay.

Chapter Six

Despite the carefully mapped-out placement of the balloons and the elaborately decorated patio and family room, which fairly sang of Ryan's affection for all things Kalico Kid, the party was really a rather informal one. There were a number of adults milling around, either catching up with one another or exchanging the kind of pleasantries that were involved when strangers attempted to become acquaintances. All the voices were raised in varying degrees in order to compete with the joyful din created by approximately ten children, each of whom sounded not unlike a small army of his or her own.

Consequently, midway through the celebration, Kara found herself the less-than-proud owner of a really raw throat. This was more shouting than she was used to, even though the people she worked with had a tendency to yell across the room to communicate.

By the time she joined in singing "Happy Birthday" with the others, she felt as if she were literally gargling with sand. Once the off-key rendition of the traditional birthday song was mercifully put out of its misery, Ryan got to make the first cut on his cake. With an eye toward saving all ten of his digits—and the fingers of those close to him—his mother quickly took over. She deftly sliced the cake, which she'd baked in the shape of the aforementioned Kalico Kid.

"Lucky thing I could get my hands on the game," Kara commented to Dave's back. Since he'd somehow managed to get in front of her and stood between her and the cake, she was about to ask him to pass her a slice when he turned around and handed her the paper plate he'd picked up.

Stunned at his thoughtfulness, she discovered that she'd temporarily lost the ability to speak. Instead, she stared. At the cake, at him.

Amused, he bent over and whispered into her ear, "Took your thunder away, didn't I?"

She wished either that he'd stop doing that, or, at the very least, that the sensation of his warm breath gliding along her skin would stop affecting her this way. "Something like that," she finally murmured.

He hadn't moved back yet. His face remained just inches away, and looking into his eyes was doing some very unexpected things to her. Things she was having a great deal of difficulty reconciling with the all-but-glaring fact that this was *Davy,* someone she'd once found irritating and annoying. Someone she'd enjoyed torturing whenever the opportunity arose—which had been often.

Unable to hear her because of the noise level, he cocked his head, pretended to cup his ear for her benefit and said, "What?"

Kara began to repeat her answer, but then, not trusting her voice to remain intact if she allowed herself to utter more than a single word, she finally gave up and merely said, "Yes."

Just then, Ryan drew all attention in his direction when, untouched cake plate in hand, he looked up plaintively toward his parents, specifically toward his mother, who, Kara had already assessed, was clearly the reigning disciplinarian of the duo.

Ryan's appeal confirmed it the next moment. "Please, Mom?"

It was obvious that Melissa had wanted to establish a little order within the chaos, or at least generate a small eye within the hurricane that was her son's birthday party. But it was equally obvious that Ryan had been drooling over his pile of gifts and wanted only to tear into the wrapping paper to unearth the treasures hidden beneath.

Melissa sighed. Her ultimate decision was never in doubt. "Okay, you can open your presents. But remember to go easy."

Kara laughed, shaking her head. "He probably didn't hear a single word she said after 'okay.'"

Kara had half expected Dave not to hear, but the look he gave her as he glanced over his shoulder was almost conspiratorial and showed her that he had and was in agreement.

Now, there's a first, she couldn't help thinking. She and Dave in agreement—and there'd been no choking involved. Would wonders never cease?

"I think he was off and running when she started to nod her head." A great deal of fondness flooded his eyes as he glanced back at Ryan. "You're only eight once."

Something in his voice piqued her interest. Kara slanted a glance toward Dave even as she watched Ryan tearing into his gifts with the innocent gusto only an eight-year-old could display.

"You actually remember being eight?" she asked him, curious.

"Vaguely," he admitted. Then he looked at her, his expression becoming more animated. "I remember you at eight."

She wasn't expecting that. Surprised, she asked, "You do? Why?"

That, as he recalled, was the year she really went to town on him. The year that she seemed determined to drive him insane. "Because you made my life a living hell that year."

Maybe she had been a little too forceful, but only because he seemed so intent on ignoring her. She'd already felt like an ugly duckling, and his treatment of her—acting as if she were invisible—was the precursor to her exacting revenge on him.

She'd implemented a lot of pranks that year. And he'd deserved every one of them, she added silently. Out loud, she apologized. But the words lacked heart.

"Sorry about that."

"No, you're not," he told her, turning to face her now. "You're grinning."

She did her best to dial it back a little, but she could feel that she was still grinning. And really enjoying herself. Her mind cast about for a good cover—and she found one.

"Just happy to be here, watching what is actually my core audience getting ecstatic over the games the company's been producing this last year," she said. To prove her point, she motioned toward Ryan.

When Dave turned around to look, he saw that his cousin's son was surrounded by a flurry of wrapping paper. The expression on the boy's face could only be described as pure rapture. The object of all this unbound excitement was now in his hands, and, Kara noted with deep satisfaction, it was the game that had initially started this particular complex ball rolling.

"Looks like our game is a hit," she murmured more to herself than to Dave.

But Dave did manage to hear her. Moreover, he looked very pleased, whether with her or himself, it wasn't clear. But he gave her shoulder a quick, reinforcing squeeze, saying, "Thanks for getting it. The look on his face is absolutely priceless."

His cousin was in obvious agreement because she seemed to be in her element, filming her son and his joyous unwrapping frenzy.

Glancing over toward him and Kara, Melissa mouthed, "Thank you," to both of them.

Kara suddenly realized that Dave had misunderstood her use of the word *our*. She'd said it referring to herself and the team she'd headed up that had done the testing and retesting of the game until they all but hated the mere mention of the title. He, obviously, had taken it on a far more personal level, which was fine for the charade they were undertaking, but not so fine if he began to believe it.

It was a problem inasmuch as she had no plans of ever being attached to anyone. She'd learned early on that the consequences of using her heart for anything other than pumping blood were daunting and came with a dark promise of being hurtful somewhere down the line. She didn't need that. *Ever.*

So instead, she concentrated strictly on Dave's cousin and smiled in response to the silent thanks, mouthing back, "Don't mention it."

Melissa's happiness at her son's joy was utterly obvious. Kara couldn't help wondering, just for a second, what that had to feel like. What was it like, having someone you'd given birth to, someone created out of a surge of love, and then nurturing that little being until it was all knees and elbows and someone you would gladly give your life for?

No point wondering, Kara told herself sternly.

Sorry, Mom, she thought, glancing in her mother's direction. *No kids for me, no grandkids for you.* She felt guilty that her mother, suddenly aware of the eye contact, smiled at her.

"Thank you, Uncle Dave!" Ryan cried as the last of the wrapping paper fell away. He dashed over and, still clutching the prized video game, threw his arms around Dave's waist.

Dave put his arms around the boy, momentarily relishing the hug before saying, "Don't thank me, Ryan.

Kara's the one who actually got her hands on the video game to bring it to you."

The fact that he was actually willing to share the glory surprised Kara. But the fact that, within less than a heartbeat, Ryan shifted his assault and threw his arms around her waist, crying, "Thank you, Aunt Kara!" surprised her even more.

She assumed that Ryan called Dave "Uncle" as a term of endearment and because there was no official title to describe their actual relationship. But calling her "Aunt" had a whole different meaning in this context. It bound her to Dave. Her natural reaction was quick and firm: deny.

"I'm not—" she began to protest, but her voice was partially drowned out by the excited squeals of Ryan's friends, who were dying to try out the game with Ryan, and partially cut off because, for such a little guy, Ryan squeezed as tightly as any metal-shop vise. He completely stole her breath away.

"Ryan, there's more," Dave coaxed, peeling back the boy's arms from around Kara's waist.

Kara tried not to be too obvious as she sucked in her first lungful of air. Dave's grin didn't help matters too much.

"Not as super as this!" the boy cried with the unabashed certainty of the very young.

"I wouldn't go betting on that, big guy," Dave warned him, a secretive smile on his face.

She looked at Dave, puzzled. Leaning into him so he could hear her, she asked Dave, "How do you know that he'll think they're cool? I mean, I know, but you don't even know what I brought," she pointed out.

He looked at her as if he was just humoring her by answering. "You work for Dynamic Video Games, don't you?" It was a rhetorical question. Or at least, it would have been, had it come from anyone but Dave.

"Yes, but how would you know if he'll even like the video games I picked for him? I mean, like I said, I know," she repeated with a casual certainty, "but isn't this a little out of your sphere of knowledge?"

Not in her wildest dreams would she have ever imagined Dave even knowing how to take a video game out of its box, much less playing one or knowing which game was the current rage. Not without help.

"Why?" he wanted to know. "Doctors play video games, too, Kara." He saw the dubious look on her face. "What, you think all I do is go to the hospital and then come home? I work in the E.R., which means that my shift can either be incredibly boring or so tense and frantic I don't get a chance to draw two breaths in succession and hope to God I made the right judgment call in a time frame where most people just have lunch." A smile played on his lips. "After a day like that, how do you think I unwind?"

"By lying in your crypt and having electrodes recharge you?" she asked innocently, keeping a straight face.

He disregarded her sarcastic reply. "I play video games."

He was serious. This was going to require a little bit of mental readjusting on her part, she decided. Kara looked at him as if she'd never met him before. Because, she thought as she took the first bite of the birthday cake he'd handed her previously, maybe she really hadn't. Apparently some people could change if they wanted to.

He could feel her eyes scrutinizing him. Delving into him as if to burrow down beneath his top layers. "Something wrong?" he wanted to know.

She shook her head, lowering her eyes back to the quickly disappearing piece of cake. "Nothing's wrong. Just trying to figure out if you're pulling my leg or not."

He took his time responding, choosing instead to let his eyes do the initial talking for him. He knew that silence, that pretending to study her, would drive her crazy.

Finally he said, "Don't worry, when I'm misaligning any part of your body, I promise that you'll be the first to know it." And then his smile widened. "Or maybe the second, but definitely one of those two numbers."

Why did that sound more like foreshadowing than a glib comment? she wondered. And why did she feel as if she'd just been placed on notice? Something hot jumped over her spine. She congratulated herself for not reacting, at least not noticeably.

Rather than answer him, she pretended to be utterly taken with the last of her slice of birthday cake and also with Ryan's revelry. He was still ripping the wrapping paper off the video games she'd bought at the company store at the last minute.

His friends cheered with each unveiling. The discovery of the Holy Grail could not have been greeted with more enthusiasm than this pint-size crowd had for these games. The shouts of encouragement and urgings to "play one of them already" were all but deafening.

Almost loud enough to drown out the special feeling growing inside of her. Unfortunately, the latter was rather overwhelming and all her attempts to ignore it were proving to be futile and useless. But she went on trying nonetheless, giving it her best shot.

Her best didn't feel nearly good enough.

Several hours later, the party began to peter out and guests left with thanks ringing in their ears and doggie bags comprised of warm leftovers placed in their hands. Kara had been elected to safeguard theirs.

Something had been weaving its way in and out of Dave's thoughts for a good part of the evening, plaguing him. He found that the answer wasn't easy and it had pushed him to teeter on a fence.

He looked at Kara somewhat uneasily as they walked down the darkened block toward his car. Unlike when they'd first arrived, there were now a great many parking spaces available. The car that had been parked behind him as well as the one that had been parked in front were gone. Pulling out was going to be easy.

Other situations remained a bit more complex.

"This isn't a real date," Dave said to her, wanting to both get her reassurance and place her on notice in case there was any sort of doubt as to what he'd signed on for. To be honest, when he'd said yes to her plan, he'd felt as if he'd been backed up against a wall. In theory, it had sounded like a good idea. In action, he wasn't so sure. Not the part about deceiving his mother—at this point she should know better than to feel a need to play covert matchmaker. What he wasn't sure about was being thrown into Kara's company time and again. It was asking for trouble.

Kara rolled her eyes. "Oh God, no. If it was a date, there'd be that first-kiss syndrome hovering over us in the background. Making us edgy."

He had no idea what she was talking about, but that was becoming par for the course. "First-kiss syndrome?" he asked. Ordinarily, he wouldn't have, feeling that by asking, he was only encouraging her. But this, he had to admit, had stirred up his curiosity. He knew he wasn't going to have any peace until she explained.

"Yes." She looked at him as they walked by a street-lamp. She couldn't believe he was actually asking. Was the man sheltered, or made out of iron? "You know what I'm talking about."

"If I did, I wouldn't be asking," he pointed out, trying to be patient.

She sighed and began to explain. "It comes packaged in a box filled with a whole bunch of anticipation. You always imagine that first kiss is going to be far better than it could possibly be so that when it finally does happen, well—" she shrugged "—it never lives up to all the preperformance hype." A glib smile played on her lips. "Kind of like most movie trailers. Anticipation embodies the very best, reality turns out to be, well—" she shrugged again, a bit more helplessly this time "—disappointing."

In his opinion, the whole process sounded much too complex and draining. For once she was the one over-thinking something. A kiss should just be spontaneous. "And this is what you go through?"

He made it sound as if he'd never experienced that first-kiss anticipation. Still, she gave him the benefit of the doubt. "Don't men go through the same thing?"

They were still within the scope of the streetlamp, not to mention that there was a full moon. Both illuminated her. His eyes swept over Kara.

For just a lingering moment, he could see himself anticipating sampling the taste of her mouth—purely on an experimental level, of course. For scientific purposes. "Well, I can't speak for most of the species, but I know I don't."

Was he that jaded? Or that innocent? It was a hard call, but with a face that Michelangelo would have been thrilled to have before him as a model, Kara had a strong feeling that it wasn't the latter.

"That's because you obviously haven't held anything in your hands that can't be found in a medical supply closet."

His mouth curved. He was not about to rise up to the bait and start citing what he *had* held that was *not* found in a medical supply closet. But he couldn't just let her challenge go completely unanswered, either. "You'd be surprised."

Her eyes met his. What would it be like to— Nope, she wasn't going to go there. She didn't care what kissing him felt like, she told herself firmly.

"Yes," she told him. "I would be."

"What do you say," he proposed, pushing a strand of hair off her forehead and tucking it behind her ear, "just for the sake of this charade, and to get it out of the way, we go through the motions of this first-kiss thing?"

She tossed her head, freeing the newly tucked strand of hair. "Syndrome."

He gave a careless, impatient shrug. "Yes, that."

"Well—" she pretended to consider "—I guess there

won't be any disappointment involved, seeing as how I'm not anticipating anything."

"A win-win situation," he replied.

She was about to ask exactly what he meant by that when he leaned in, took her face in his hands and then pressed his lips against hers.

She was expecting something simple and braced herself for the usual disappointment. Though what came next was anything but disappointing.

Chapter Seven

Her skin on fire, her mind gone, Kara could feel herself free-falling.

Or was she actually just leaning into him as she desperately attempted to absorb every beat, every nuance of whatever this was that was happening?

And all because Dave had upped the ante, increasing the depth and scope of what had been, up until this very moment, a cherished if somewhat disappointing ritual.

This wasn't even a real date, for pity's sake. The realization drummed through her head and then vanished.

Maybe, Dave thought, he was just trying to get this over with. Or maybe, his ego battered, he was attempting to teach the brat from his childhood a lesson not to write him off so cavalierly.

It might have started out being a little bit of both.

He really didn't know, couldn't remember. What he did know was that he could almost literally *feel* his blood rushing madly through his body. Could feel a cache of needs suddenly come spilling out, tumbling to the foreground. All while his head was spinning like an old-fashioned top, snatching away his breath, not to mention his better judgment. Hell, snatching away any kind of judgment at all. Because if he'd had a shred of that left, he would have backed away.

Instead, rather than fleeing, he was moving forward, reaching out for the mind-scrambling experience—and for her—so that he could continue this. Whatever the hell *this* was.

The closest thing he could liken it to was being drunk. He'd been in that state only once before and had vowed never to be like that again. He didn't enjoy the feeling nor the fact that he was not in control of his own actions.

Just the way, Dave realized with a start, he wasn't in control now. And though that deeply offended his sense of order, the rush kissing this woman created was instantly, incredibly, completely addictive.

All he could think of was getting more. And that there had to be a way to make it never stop.

Those desires and passions that had risen up within him were demanding he do something about them. Demanding that he explore exactly what it was that this otherwise exceedingly irritating woman with a face like a mischievous angel and a body that could lead a man happily to sin was doing to him. Then do it back to her. In spades.

But the edge of his cousin's block was not the place to find out, his common sense insisted.

And so, even though his body was begging for satisfaction, Dave summoned every ounce of strength within him and abruptly pulled his head back. He was surprised that his neck didn't snap.

He saw confusion and wonder in Kara's bright blue eyes—why hadn't he ever noticed how blue her eyes were before? They seemed to delve into him and go beneath all the layers he'd carefully placed between himself and the world, leaving him not just naked but in the state he hated most of all.

Vulnerable.

He did his best to sound nonchalant, as if his insides were not still on fire. "Well, we got that out of the way."

The words hit her like a water balloon, and it took Kara a second to find her tongue. And then another second more to remember words and how to form them.

"Yes," she agreed, her throat so tight it was almost choking her, "we did."

Didn't you feel *anything, you bum?* her mind screamed.

She felt as if she'd been fried to an absolute crisp, and he looked as if he'd endured something necessary, but annoying, like an inoculation against the flu.

Because she had a very uneasy feeling that she might fall over and pass out if she didn't get in more than a trickle of oxygen, Kara drew in a deep breath as covertly as possible. It helped.

A little.

Stealing a look at Dave to see if he was the *least* bit rattled, she felt the bitter bite of disappointment.

And then she thought she saw a bead of sweat at his temple. Unless the man had suddenly come down with a fever—and even that could act in her favor—the bead of sweat meant that she had gotten to him.

It seemed only fair since he had gotten to her. Bigtime. Not that she was ever, *ever* going to admit that to him. Not even under penalty of death, she tacked on silently.

If she did, she *knew* it would lead to her undoing because the man would take to crowing about it and he would be utterly insufferable. Even more than he was right now, Kara added.

And then he completely blew her away by asking, "Want to test-drive another one, in case the first kiss was just a fluke?"

He asked the question with no more emotion than if he were inquiring how she liked her eggs.

What she didn't realize was that he was trying his very best to sound as nonchalant as possible. In reality, he was anything but. So much so that he doubted if he was actually fooling her.

She saw the uneasiness in his eyes. That trumped anything he had to say. It was at that moment that she knew she'd gotten to him.

Lifting her face up to his, a grin played along her lips as another, stronger dose of anticipation—this time fueled by knowledge—raced through her.

"I was always game for anything," Kara reminded him, her eyes dancing.

That she was, he recalled. But he hadn't been, especially not back then. He'd played it safe.

He didn't want to play it safe now.

Dave slipped his arms around her and drew her to him ever so carefully. "I remember," he replied, his voice low, his mind already trying to figure out how to survive the turbulent ride looming ahead.

Part of him was fervently hoping that the impact of that first kiss was, for some unknown reason, all in his imagination.

Part of him was hoping it hadn't been.

Back away. Now! something in his head screamed, and maybe he would have, except for the fact that the smile on her lips was daring him. Silently issuing a challenge.

God help him, he could never walk away from one of her challenges, even when he knew it was going to turn out badly for him. It was as if he was determined to prove something. Back then it was that he was at least as manly as she was, if not more. Now it was...

It was...

Hell, he didn't know what it was or why he was doing this, only that he *had* to.

He had no choice.

It wasn't a mistake, wasn't a temporary foray into insanity, Kara thought as the impact of his mouth on hers hit her with the force of an exploding grenade. The next moment, she was lamenting the very same thing she'd just been glorying in. Because a tiny drop of common sense had returned and found her.

Why, of all the times she'd been in this situation, anticipating a first kiss and being so sadly disappointed moments later when there was no magic, did she have to feel it now?

Why *this* man of all men, for heaven's sake?

Maybe because secretly, I always had a crush on him. Maybe, all this time, I've known that was the case and tucked it away in my heart.

Or maybe I'm just a glutton for punishment.

And the next moment, she didn't know anything—except that this kiss was even better than the first one. That was something she would have said was utterly impossible—if she weren't in the midst of experiencing it right now.

Every fiber of her being was melting into a puddle at his feet.

"Hey, you two, get a room!"

The glib comment, coming out of nowhere and followed by a chuckle, made Kara's heart slam against her rib cage as she all but leaped away from Dave.

She was behaving like some inexperienced adolescent who was guilty of misconduct. Behaving like someone she didn't know.

A lot of that going around, Kara thought, upbraiding herself.

She was extremely annoyed, though more with herself than with Dave. But he wasn't blameless in this, she thought, upset.

As her mental fog began to clear, Kara found herself looking up into the face of one of the party guests—a friend of Ryan's father. If it wasn't bad enough that he'd stumbled upon them in this compromising situation, the man was a priest to boot.

Despite the situation—or maybe because of it—there was a genial expression on the man's face.

"Just so you know," he told them, claiming the last car, located at the end of the block, "I'm available for impromptu weddings." He punctuated his offer with a broad wink.

"We'll keep that in mind," Dave replied a little stiffly.

Now *that* was the Dave she remembered and knew, Kara thought. The one who acted as if he had a pointy stick strategically positioned where the sun didn't shine. Not the one who brought her blood up past the boiling point without even trying.

Forcing a smile to her lips, Kara tried to look relaxed.

"Nice to have met you, Father," she said, referring to earlier at the party, hoping to get the focus off the present and the fact that he had found them hermetically sealed to one another.

"Same here," he told her, taking her hand in both of his and shaking it. There was a definite twinkle in his eyes, visible even in the limited light. "I look forward to seeing you again," he added, then his eyes shifted to include Dave. "Both of you."

Dave had no choice but to nod. After all, the priest had just stumbled across them bringing new meaning to the term *kissing*.

"See you around, Father Jack," Dave said, hoping to urge the man along his way.

"I can only hope." Father Jack chuckled as he got into his vehicle and then closed the door.

The moment mercifully interrupted, Dave did his best to view it as a last-minute reprieve. With that in mind, he shoved the incident behind him and out of sight.

"C'mon," he said to Kara gruffly, "I'll take you home."

Home.

Kara nodded, deciding it was best if she didn't speak just yet. Everything inside of her was still trembling, and she wanted to wait until it calmed down a little before trying to form words that made sense.

Because right now, she was feeling anything but sensible.

If she had been, she wouldn't have been hoping that by taking her "home" Dave had meant he intended to continue what had been so suddenly interrupted.

Because she wanted to make love with him.

She upbraided herself again. What the hell was wrong with her, anyway? This was Dave. Dave, who had been as squeamish as she had been reckless and brave, handling the slimy critters he wouldn't pick up and then finding ways to torture him with them.

Kara stared straight ahead into the night, concentrating on getting herself under control. Beside her, she heard Dave put his key into the ignition and assumed they would be on their way in a moment.

The moment came and went, but they didn't.

She looked at him. His profile was rigid. Now what? "Something wrong?" she asked.

Dave didn't answer her. Instead, he turned his key again—and received the same exact results.

Nothing.

She heard him let out a long, deep, frustrated sigh. She waited for the obligatory curse words, but there were none. Impressed, she watched him in silence.

He gave starting the car a third try, this time with his

foot on the accelerator, pressing down hard. A horrible sound pierced the night air, but his attempt made no difference. The vehicle wasn't moving and had slipped into silence.

Her first thought was that Dave had run out of gas, and she glanced at the dashboard just in case. But the gauge claimed that there was over three-quarters of a tank still available.

Dave saw where she was looking and said with barely reined-in irritation, "No, I didn't forget to put gas in."

"Never hurts to check," she told him cheerfully. She unbuckled her seat belt and got out of the car.

"Where are you going?" he asked.

"Nowhere, apparently," she commented, frowning at the front of his sports car. "Pop the hood." Her instruction was accompanied by a hand gesture aimed upward.

She was nothing if not animated, Dave thought. But instead of doing as she said, he started to get out of the car. Maybe he could help.

"No." The single word snapped out of her mouth, sounding far too much like an order to please him. "Stay inside the car," she told him. "I need you to pop the hood and then turn the key for me."

Dave bristled. This wasn't the way it was supposed to be, he thought, annoyed not so much with her as with his own lack of expertise when it came to things with engines and tires. He was the guy, damn it. He was supposed to be the one standing out there, issuing orders to her as he tried to diagnose what was wrong with the damn car. Their relationship was too new to be behaving like this.

He bit off a couple of words, swallowing them instead. When it came to cars, he had never had either the time or the interest to learn what it was that made them tick.

Or not tick.

"Pop the hood," she instructed again, looking at him expectantly. When he didn't comply, she came back to the driver's side and peered into the car. "What's the matter? Why aren't you popping the hood like I told you to?"

He would, if he knew where the hood release was. The fact that he didn't just served to make him feel even more inept. Ordinarily his lack of experience in these matters didn't bother him, but it did this time. Because this was Kara.

"Um…"

Kara realized what the problem was. She moved closer to the driver's side, opened the door and leaned in to feel around the area beneath and to the left of the steering wheel. Per force she had to brush up against his leg. When she made contact, she flashed him a grin.

"I'm not getting fresh," she told him innocently. "Your knee's in the same area as the hood release." Feeling around for the lever as Dave tried to shift his knee away from her, she finally located it. "Ah, here it is," she declared with triumph.

She pulled the lever, then returned to the front of the car, where she lifted and secured the hood.

"Okay," she called out. "Turn the key for me. Please."

He did, and this time he thought he heard what sounded like a slight cough coming from his engine. Praying that it had caught, Dave began to pump the pedal, giving the engine what he thought it needed: more gas.

"Stop!" Kara cried. "You'll flood the engine." Peering around the side of the car, she asked him, "Do you have a flashlight in the glove compartment? I think I know the problem. If I'm right, we can be on the road in about fifteen minutes."

"Sounds good to me," he said, his voice somewhat wooden. The moment was long gone. Just as well. He opened up his glove compartment and took out a small, sleek flashlight. Shifting, he leaned over in his seat and offered it to Kara.

"Okay, let's see if I can get us rolling," she murmured, getting down to business.

He knew he should be relieved, for a number of reasons, that they'd be parting ways soon.

But he wasn't.

Chapter Eight

"Where did you learn how to fix cars?"

Dave's question surprised her as it broke the silence that had filled the interior of his car. She had all but given up hope that he'd utter a single word before dropping her off at her apartment, and she'd be damned if she was going to be the first one to say anything. It wasn't her fault that she knew how to fix cars and he didn't. It wasn't in her nature to play the helpless female when she wasn't any such thing.

"So you *can* talk." Kara shifted in her seat to look at him. "I thought that maybe you'd suddenly been struck mute. To answer your question," she continued, "my dad was a car enthusiast. He loved taking engines apart, restoring old cars. He was never happier than when he was fixing some kind of engine problem, getting it to run more efficiently," she recalled fondly.

It seemed like a million years ago now. Neil Calhoun had been gone for thirteen years, succumbing to the disease that had ravaged him the summer she turned seventeen. She still missed him like crazy. Especially whenever she tinkered with a car.

"When my dad wasn't at work, he was in the garage, working on a car. I wanted to spend time with him, so I pretended to be interested in cars." Her mouth curved. "After a while, I didn't have to pretend."

Dave wondered if she was aware of the irony of what she'd just said—that she'd gone through the motions of a pretense until it no longer was a pretense.

Not wanting to get embroiled in a potential argument—he knew when he was outmatched—he decided not to bring it up. Instead, he focused on Kara's initial glib comment regarding his silence.

"I wasn't struck mute," Dave informed her grudgingly. "It's just that…" His voice trailed off as he realized that there was no ego-saving way to finish his sentence.

"Having me fix the car when you didn't have a clue what was wrong made you feel less than a man?" Kara supplied.

Dave was prepared to go one round with her, expecting some sarcastic comment about his manhood or lack thereof, but again, just like with the kiss and with Gary at the free clinic, she surprised him. This time by not trying to humiliate him the way she would have done when they were kids. Reluctantly, he nodded.

"It shouldn't have," she said. He continued waiting for the punch line. There wasn't any. "Lots of guys don't know their way around a car. And everybody has their strengths and weaknesses. Yours is fixing people. Me, I can generally figure out what's wrong with a car. In the grand scheme of things, yours is the more important skill."

For a second, he was tempted to ask to see some identification. This was *not* the Kara Calhoun he'd known. That one would have filleted him with her razor-sharp tongue before he could even think of a way to defend himself.

Still not completely at ease, Dave did begin to relax just a little more. Enough to ask, "What's your weakness?"

The question caught her off guard. Kara blinked. "Excuse me?"

"You just said that everyone's got a weakness," he reminded her. She had succeeded in arousing his curiosity. "So what's yours?"

"I should have said everybody *but* me." She could feel him waiting for her to give a real answer. After a moment, she shrugged. Still looking out through the front windshield, she said, "I can't cook."

"I can." It would have been difficult, growing up in an Italian home, not picking up a few pointers. His mother, perhaps because he was an only child and she had no daughter to share things with, had made sure he knew all the basics when it came to finding his way around the kitchen.

She heard him laugh shortly to himself. "What?"

"Nothing." But then he went on to say, "It's just that I'd say we complement each other."

"Not without some severe arm twisting," Kara countered. But her mouth was soft as she said it, giving way to a smile at the end.

He spared her a look just as he made a right turn and approached her apartment complex. She'd changed, he thought. She had never smiled like that when she was younger. It was a warm, inviting smile. Made a man let his guard down.

"Maybe not so severe," he commented.

She wanted to deny his assumption, but she couldn't manage to do it. Lost for a retort, she fell back on another shrug.

"Anyway," she began, shifting topics, "I think we pulled off the first leg of our plan pretty well. Both your mother and mine looked as if they bought into our fledgling romance."

For a moment back there, under the streetlamp, so had he. The power of suggestion was a dangerous, scary thing, Dave thought.

"First leg," he repeated, turning his car into her complex. He headed for guest parking. Kara really had put a lot of planning into this, he thought. "Are we talking about a two-legged creature, a four-legged one, an octopus or a centipede?"

Knowing it was going to take more than just one more shot, she went with the second choice. "The four-legged kind," she said.

Okay, he supposed that sounded reasonable. He'd been worried that she'd want to go on with this charade for several months. "And the second leg is?"

"Just letting our mothers see us out and about." They were going to have to be noticeable, but not obvious, which was tricky. Too obvious and her mother would definitely see through the plan, ruining everything. Not obvious enough and what was the point? "I'll see about coming up with a list of places and activities where one or both of the dynamic duo would be sure to see us."

"'Dynamic duo'?" he repeated, confused. "What do Batman and Robin have to do with all this?"

"Nothing." She saw the confusion on his face. Kara sighed. "I forgot how literal you could be."

How the hell else was he supposed to take her comment? "And I forgot how you hardly ever made any sense."

"To *you*," she emphasized. "Nobody else ever has trouble getting my meaning."

He highly doubted that. "Do you visit an alternate universe often?"

"A joke." Kara splayed her hand across her chest, as if to press back a heart attack brought on by shock. "Wow, maybe there is hope for you yet," she said with an easy smile. "And for the record, the dynamic duo in this case refers to—"

"—our mothers, yes. I get it."

She patted him on the shoulder, a teacher proud of her slow but determined student.

"Doesn't matter how slow your mind works, Dave, as long as it eventually comes through." She was surprised when he started to get out on his side. "Where are you going?" she asked with just the slightest hint of wariness in her voice.

Slight or not, Dave picked up on it and it changed all the ground rules. She'd looked flustered for that one unguarded second. She was afraid, he realized. Afraid that he was inviting himself over. It wasn't hard to figure out what she was thinking after that. That, once inside her apartment, he'd try to press his advantage.

The thought placed the ball back in his court, making him far less leery and a great deal more relaxed. "Your father taught you how to work on cars, mine taught me that you always walk a lady to her door after a date." A smile played along his lips. "I guess that would apply to you, too."

"Very funny," she answered. "So about our next 'date,' I think I've got the perfect place. Our mothers have a standing date for the Orange County fair each year—the first Saturday the fair's open. That's this coming Saturday." Her grin was wide. "I thought we'd join them." Then it faded a little as she said, "It'll require lots of hand holding. Are you up to it?"

He wasn't twelve anymore. There was no stigma attached to holding a girl's hand. Even hers.

"If I have to, I have to," he replied, trying to sound convincingly put out.

But the parameters had changed suddenly and drastically with that experimental "first-kiss syndrome" she'd sprung on him. He knew now that he never should have proposed "getting it out of the way." It was far better to be attracted to her and wonder if there was anything to the attraction than to actually go through the steps and find out.

Because now there was no room for doubt. He *was* attracted to her. A great deal.

And that, he knew, was definitely going to be a problem, at least for one of them.

"I'll get my shots," he said as they came to a stop before her front door.

"You do that," she told him. Getting her key out, she paused before putting it into the lock. "You don't want to come inside, do you?"

Actually, he did. Very much so. Which was why he couldn't.

"I'd better be getting back," he told her evasively, not answering outright. "I've got an early shift tomorrow," he tacked on for good measure.

She nodded. Relieved.

And yet...

There is no "yet," Kara silently argued. If she was feeling anything, it was just her, throwing herself into this part. There was nothing between them and there wasn't going to be. If she was lucky, she would get through this charade intact without giving in to the temptation of killing the man. She knew it was just a matter of time before the desire to put him out of her misery returned to tempt her mercilessly.

"Okay, then, I'll be in touch." She saw the look of surprise on his face. "About the fair," she prompted. Had he forgotten already?

"Oh, right. Okay."

It was time for him to get moving, Dave told himself. Time to point his feet toward his car and start walking back to guest parking. Why he felt as if he'd just stepped into glue that was holding him fast was something he didn't quite understand. It couldn't be because he wanted to remain in her company for a couple more minutes, that would be too ridiculous for words.

So why was there no other part of him moving except for his lips? "Um, thanks again for getting that game for Ryan."

"You don't have to thank me," she told him, and she meant it. Then, before Dave could respond, she added, "The look on Ryan's face was thanks enough."

Goose bumps were beginning to claim her flesh, traveling up and down the length of her bare arms. She blamed it on the night air, although it really wasn't all that cool.

"See you," she said cheerfully, then launched herself into her apartment and shut the door behind her before she did something stupid, like pull him in after her. Or kiss him again.

Dave stood there on her doorstep, looking at the closed door for several moments. For a split second, he contemplated knocking and asking to come in under some pretext or other. But then decided against it.

He'd been up too long and sleep deprivation was making his mind wander into strange, incomprehensible areas, tempting him to go against his own better instincts. Never mind that while in medical school and then during residency, he'd pulled back-to-back-to-back shifts that would have worn out the average robot. This was his excuse and he was sticking to it.

"See you around," he said to the door and then turned and walked away.

Kara had remained on the other side of the door, torn. Listening. Aware that he hadn't walked away and struggling with the very strong temptation of opening the door and pulling him in. Only the realization that it would have been a very huge mistake kept her from doing it.

The future, from where she stood, looked a little rocky. Of course, she could just decide to abandon this whole charade, but she knew that her mother was not about to give up now that she'd gotten her toes wet in matchmaking waters.

She might not be aware of any biological clock ticking, but apparently her mother, somehow newly equipped with super-hearing, was. And if her mother wasn't stopped in her tracks now, who knew who the next candidate she came up with might be? Better to nip this in the bud now.

All of this angst would be moot if only kissing Dave had been like rubbing her lips along a dead fish. Then all her problems would have been solved and she wouldn't be feeling as attracted to him as she was.

"Oh well, like the flu, this too shall pass," she told herself out loud.

For the time being, though, she forced herself to put it out of her mind.

"So it's working," Lisa declared.

The minute she'd walked into her house, the phone had started ringing. It was no surprise that Paulette was on the other end of the line. Paulette always did have timing down to a science, and this time she was calling, Lisa assumed, to crow about how successful her plan to get their children together had turned out.

"Of course it's working," Paulette answered with no small display of confidence. "I knew it would. Kara wants to teach me a lesson. I mean, teach *us* a lesson."

This, Lisa thought, had to be the fastest that Paulette had ever lost her. "Excuse me?"

Paulette laughed and proceeded to explain. "I know my daughter. She has this radar that puts her on the alert if something is a little off. In this case, the request for that game tipped her off."

"But Ryan really wanted it," Lisa pointed out. That hadn't been a ruse. "You saw his reaction at the party when he unwrapped it. He was overjoyed."

"Yes, but you have to admit that my coming out and asking Kara to deliver the game to Dave at the clinic because it was closer for her than for me was rather obvious."

Lisa had thought that herself initially, but her friend's enthusiasm had made her overlook that point. "If it was that obvious and you knew that she was going to see right through it, why did you do it?"

"Because I knew she'd react this way."

She could hear the smile in Paulette's voice. "What way?" she asked, frustrated. "You know, until this minute, I didn't think I was in jeopardy of coming down with Alzheimer's so early, but now I'm not so sure I'm not already mired in it." Drawing in a long breath, Lisa braced herself. "Paulette, what are you talking about? I'm not following you."

"I know it sounds kind of involved," Paulette allowed patiently, "but neither one of us has simple kids. Consequently, we're engaged in a mental chess game. The only way to get Kara and Dave together is to make them want to outsmart us. Challenge them. Especially Kara. And I was right."

If you say so, Lisa thought. Out loud she asked, "Okay, so do you have any idea what they think they're doing?"

"Does spring follow winter?" Paulette asked.

"With you I wouldn't bet on it," Lisa answered.

Paulette laughed. "Our kids are pretending to hit it off so that eventually they can break up dramatically—undoubtedly somewhere within our hearing range. The thought behind that—I'd stake my life on it—is that we will feel so bad that things didn't work out between them and that they wound up in emotional pain because of us, we'll swear off meddling in their affairs for the rest of their lives."

"In other words, once this little three-act play is over, we'll be back to square one and they'll be no closer to a relationship with each other—or anyone else—than they were when we started," Lisa concluded glumly.

She was about to ask what the point of going through these paces was if that was to be the outcome, but she never got the chance.

Paulette laughed quietly at the summation. "Not if I'm right."

Lisa sighed. "Okay, I admit it. I'm the slow one," she said, not believing it for a minute. "You're going to have to explain what you mean by that."

"What I'm counting on is that they're both going to get so involved in pretending to fall in love, they won't see it coming."

Exasperated, Lisa enunciated each word slowly. "See *what* coming?"

"That they really are falling in love."

Paulette was taking a great deal for granted here, Lisa thought. She wasn't nearly as confident about the outcome as her best friend seemed to be. "And you think this is a sure thing."

"Yes," Paulette cried with feeling. "They're perfect for each other. We both know they are. Besides, I saw the way they looked at each other when one thought that the other wasn't looking. There's definite electricity going on there."

"Hopefully not enough to kill them," Lisa murmured under her breath.

"Okay, I can see you definitely need convincing. I was saving this for last." She paused for effect, then delivered her crowning glory. "Father Jack saw them."

It was, Lisa decided, like pulling teeth. Except that Paulette really seemed to be enjoying this. "Saw them what, Paulette? Saw them what?"

"He saw them kissing. Your son was kissing my daughter. Or my daughter was kissing your son. Either way, lips were locked, and there was no one around to serve as an audience. Which meant they were acting on their feelings, not putting on a show for us."

Lisa wasn't so quick to celebrate. She'd always been the more practical one in their friendship. "Maybe they thought there was an audience. Or maybe they were practicing."

It was obvious that Paulette didn't think either point was valid, but she let them slide, saying, "I don't care what the excuse is, as long as they wind up in love. You look best in green, by the way."

That had come out of nowhere. "Thank you, but why are you telling me this?"

"So that you know what color dress to wear for the wedding," Paulette explained cheerfully. "A mint-green dress. Cocktail length," she added. "I'll wear baby blue."

Lisa could only laugh. There was no arguing with Paulette when she got like this. All she could do was go along with it and fervently pray that her friend was ultimately right. Because she really did want to see Dave and Kara together.

Chapter Nine

The doorbell rang.

Damn it, he's early. Figures.

Luckily, this time so was she.

Nonetheless, Kara felt her pulse flutter a beat before she opened her front door. She told herself she was being stupid. This was Dave, someone she'd technically known for most of her life. When she got right down to it, she couldn't remember *not* knowing him.

Nothing had changed, she argued silently, except maybe that he'd gotten taller, but then, so had she. Increased height was absolutely no reason for her pulse to skip a beat.

Stepping back, she opened the door wider. Dave was on her doorstep, looking ruggedly handsome in jeans and a Wedgwood-blue T-shirt—did he know that was her favorite color?

Oh, c'mon, Kara, how could he know that?

There was also an odd expression on his face as he looked at her. Was it just her, or was it getting warmer? The weatherman hadn't said anything about breaking records today. But there was no denying that she certainly felt hot.

"You're staring," she admonished.

Damn it, he was, Dave upbraided himself. But she was wearing denim shorts. Incredibly short denim shorts—and had somehow managed to grow several more inches of leg than he remembered her having. The icy-blue halter top that accented her taut midriff and small waist didn't exactly help keep his body temperature down any, either. Where was it written that skinny little brats could grow up to be sexy as hell?

Dave blinked to clear his head and refocus his eyes. "Sorry," he murmured, "didn't realize I was staring. I didn't get much sleep last night."

"Anticipating our date?" Kara asked cheerfully, tongue-in-cheek.

Or, at least, she meant for him to *think* she was being flippant. Truth was, she'd had less than her usual amount of sleep herself for that very reason. She told herself it was because she wanted to pull this off properly in order to ultimately teach her mother and his a lesson, but there was a part of her that wasn't really buying her own excuse. There was something about Dave, this new, improved model, that was definitely getting to her. Especially after she'd made the mistake of locking lips with him. Now all she seemed to do was think about that kiss. It was definitely getting in the way of her being her blasé self.

"Extra shift at the E.R.," he told her. It was a white lie, but there was no way for her to check that out and it was a handy enough excuse to hide behind. He hadn't counted on her reacting with concern.

"You want to reschedule?" Kara asked him. He expected her to say something like "Gotcha!" but she looked dead serious. "The fair's here for another twenty-eight days."

No, he didn't want to reschedule. For a number of reasons. Not the least of which was that he'd psyched himself up to spend the afternoon and possibly the evening as well in her company.

He had no idea how she would react if he admitted that to her—most likely it would result in her torturing him one way or another—so instead he said crisply, "Don't want it hanging over my head."

Her smile slipped away. "Fine," she retorted.

Served her right for trying to be thoughtful and put his needs first. Things like that were just wasted on someone like Dave. "By all means, let's get this over with."

She grabbed her oversize purse and walked out in front of him.

Giving him what amounted to the best view he'd had in a very long while.

Half an hour later, thanks to a decrease in morning traffic, they were meeting both their mothers at the entrance to the fairgrounds.

The two women were already there, waiting for them, which came as no surprise to Kara. She'd expected as much. Her mother waved with the enthusiasm of an Indy 500 starter signaling the beginning of the famous race.

May the better side win, Kara said to herself, smiling at the two women.

"Lisa and I talked about it, and we don't want you two to hang back just for us. Enjoy yourselves," she urged with feeling. "Take in some of the rides. You'll make more progress without us tagging along, dragging you down. We can all meet for lunch," Paulette suggested, going on to name one of the booths specializing in barbecued spare ribs and a few other things guaranteed to make a cardiologist weep. "Say about one?" She looked over her shoulder at Lisa for confirmation.

"One's fine with me," Lisa responded, picking up her cue. She smiled at Kara, then at her son. "How about you two?"

"Whatever you want, Mom," Dave replied. The easygoing response had Paulette smiling as she looked back at her best friend.

"I always thought he was such a good boy."

Kara felt herself bristling. "Mom, in case you haven't noticed, Dave's not a little boy anymore. He's grown up. We both have," she emphasized. That she was suddenly championing Dave surprised even her.

Her mother looked completely unfazed by her argument. "Doesn't matter how old you get," the woman maintained. "You'll always be my kid."

Kara rolled her eyes, then turned toward Dave, who was acting like a spectator rather than a participant, she thought irritably. She took his side, why wasn't he taking hers?

"Why do I feel as if I've just had a curse placed on me?" she asked wryly.

Her mother seemed to take no offense. "Because you're as rebellious as I was at your age. Takes standing on this side of parenthood to understand what I'm feeling." There was deep affection in her eyes as she ran her hand along her daughter's cheek. "You will someday," she predicted. Then, reverting back to her bubbly self, she concluded, "Until then, go, have fun."

"You're being kind of hard on her, don't you think?" Dave asked once they were walking away from their mothers.

She didn't like him pointing out her faults, especially when it seemed as if he was taking her mother's side. "Did it ever occur to you that I might have to be? If I'm not, she'll have me in a bib, a bonnet and a high chair in under an hour."

He moved slightly to the side to avoid a group of five heading in another direction. The fairgrounds were already fairly crowded, he noted. "If that were the case," he pointed out, "she wouldn't be trying to get us together for the purpose of marriage, now, would she?"

Kara frowned. She might have known that Dave would be perverse. "Well, I can see why she likes you so much. I'm surprised my mother thinks that I'm good enough for you."

He moved behind her, taking her arm to avoid walking into two teens busy texting, their eyes glued to their cell phone screens. Electronics should be banned in certain places, he thought.

"And I can see why you have trouble getting dates with that winning personality of yours."

Her back went up instantly. "I get asked out plenty, thank you."

"So why aren't you with someone?" His eyes pinned her. "You're certainly attractive enough."

"I could ask you the same thing," she declared tersely, then did a mental double take as Dave's second sentence registered in her head. "What did you just say?"

Dave obliged and repeated, "Why aren't you with someone?"

Kara shook her head. "No, not that. The other part."

He knew what she was referring to the first time around, but decided to draw this out, curious to see her response. "You have a mirror, you know what you look like."

This caught her completely off guard. "You think I'm attractive?"

The last time he'd said anything about her looks, he'd said she had a face that not even a frog would want. He'd been eleven at the time and she'd just put a red-striped ribbon snake on his shoulder. He didn't know they were harmless and it had scared the hell out of him until he heard her laughing. He'd been furious.

Maybe he'd said too much, he thought. Still, she really was a knockout. Especially in that outfit. "What I think doesn't matter. Certain things are just self-evident."

What did she say to something like that? If she thanked him, she might discover that it was all a gag. But if he was serious, then shouldn't she say something?

Kara shook her head. "I have no idea what to make of you."

She saw the corners of his mouth curve. "Good. It goes both ways." Dave looked out on the fairgrounds. "So, what do you want to go on first? How about the Ferris wheel?" he suggested since they were standing only a few feet away from the ride.

She didn't answer him immediately, which was highly unusual for her. Ordinarily, no one could get her to stop talking. At least, that was the case with the Kara he remembered.

Looking at her more closely, he noticed that she seemed uncomfortable. What was that all about? he wondered.

"What?" he prodded. "You don't like riding on Ferris wheels?"

"They're fine," she retorted a little too quickly and a little too forcefully. "C'mon," she declared, looking for all the world like someone who had made up her mind to face a firing squad with bravado. "Let's go."

"Wait a second." Grabbing her arm, he pulled her back and held her in place. He knew that look in her eyes. That was definitely fear. He put two and two together. "Are you afraid of heights?"

"No!" she cried angrily.

"You are, aren't you?" It seemed incredible. She'd always been fearless to the point of being reckless. He tried to make sense of it. "But you used to climb trees like a monkey."

She frowned, turning away. When he looked at her, she felt as if he could see right into her. "Very flattering image."

She wasn't denying it, which meant he'd guessed right. "What happened to change that?"

She shrugged, still avoiding his eyes. "I found out I can't fly."

The woman had to learn how not to talk in code. "Care to explain that?"

She looked at him resentfully. Why was he poking at her sore points? She hated admitting a weakness. Hated being shackled by fears. "I fell out of a tree, okay? I've been a little leery of high places ever since then. Satisfied?" she challenged.

"Okay, we don't have to go on the Ferris wheel."

Oh no, she wasn't falling for that trap. "What? And have you hold it over me? No, thank you. We *are* going on the Ferris wheel." Grabbing his hand, she pulled him after her as she deliberately walked toward the end of the line for the ride.

She didn't get very far because he wasn't about to allow himself to be dragged along. "What are you, twelve? If you're afraid to go on, we don't have to go on. Plenty of other things to do here. It's not like it's the only ride."

She was not going to wimp out. Kara was determined to be brave.

"I'm facing my fears," she announced between clenched teeth. But despite her yanking at his arm, he wasn't budging. "Now what?" she demanded.

"I changed my mind." His tone was simple, but anyone could see he was not a man who was about to be budged. "I don't want to go on the Ferris wheel."

She began to say something terse, then relented.

Maybe this was his way of giving her a way out. She let go of his arm and stepped back to look at him.

"You know," she began slowly, almost shyly, "if I didn't know any better, I'd say you were being nice."

Dave looked at her, and the moment felt strung out in time, moving toward infinity. It didn't help. All he could think about was her. About the way her lips had felt beneath his. The way her body, all soft curves, had yielded against his.

Damn if he didn't feel a pull within him. With effort, Dave shut out the surge of desire that threatened to overrun him.

"But you know better, don't you?" he asked quietly.

Before she could answer, they heard someone screaming for help. Turning, they saw a distraught-looking woman running in their general direction with a child in her arms. The little boy—he couldn't have been any older than six—was bleeding from a gash on his forehead. His eyes, usually the liveliest part of a boy's face, were shut.

"Help me!" the woman cried desperately as she ran, looking around wildly. "Someone please help me!"

Before Kara could do anything, Dave quickly moved in front of the woman, causing her to stop in her tracks.

"I'm a doctor," he told her, his eyes never leaving hers. "Can you tell me what happened?" His voice was calm, soothing, in order to pull the woman back from the brink of hysteria.

Suddenly, the woman all but melted before him, her legs giving way as if they couldn't support her any longer. Dave caught the little boy before she could drop him. At the same time, Kara grabbed the woman, keeping her reasonably upright.

"It's okay, I've got you," she told the woman, doing her best to mimic Dave's tone. "Tell us what happened," she repeated.

By now people were beginning to gather around them, drawn by the woman's cries and the drama that was unfolding.

The woman looked at them, wild-eyed, as if she couldn't believe what was happening herself. "He was running ahead of me and he tripped and hit his head on the side of a cart. I told him not to run, I *told* him," she insisted frantically.

"Kids don't always listen," Dave assured her, his voice still low. He needed to keep her talking. "Go on," he urged while he continued working on the boy, pressing a clean handkerchief against the gash on his forehead.

The woman swallowed. She was beginning to shake. She was going into shock, Dave thought.

"There was so much blood." Her eyes filled with tears. "When I got to him, he wasn't moving. I can't get him to open his eyes. Why can't I get him to open his eyes?" she demanded hysterically, her voice cracking as she looked to Dave for an answer.

But it was Kara who answered her. "It's going to be all right." She continued holding on to the woman. Her voice was low, comforting. Unshakable. "Don't worry, he's in very good hands."

As she said it, she looked at Dave, silently raising an eyebrow, waiting for him to say something. He'd placed the boy down on the grass on his back and was checking him for a pulse. The slight nod told Kara he'd found it.

Glancing up at the woman, he asked, "What's your son's name, ma'am?"

It took her a moment to pull her thoughts together. "Um, Kyle. His name's Kyle. Kyle Taylor." Her breathing was growing erratic. "Is he going to be all right?"

"He's going to be fine," Kara assured her, cutting in, afraid that Dave would say something practical and conservative, hedging his bets. It wasn't something the woman was up to hearing. "You have to calm down," she told her. "He's going to need his mom to be there for him when he opens his eyes."

The woman hiccuped, as if repressing a flood of tears, then nodded.

"All right," she murmured. "All right." Her eyes never left her son's inert body on the ground.

Dave pulled out his cell phone. Tucking it against his shoulder and neck, he quickly placed a call for an ambulance while he worked to stop the blood from oozing out of the boy's head wound.

"Wake up, baby, please wake up," the woman begged her unconscious son. The boy's eyes remained closed, and the woman's panic grew.

The paramedics arrived within minutes. In short order, the boy was strapped onto a gurney and placed inside the rear of the ambulance, his mother beside him.

"Maybe you'd better come along with us, Doc," one of the paramedics suggested. It was obvious from his manner that he knew Dave. "We're short an EMT this run."

Under normal circumstances, Dave would have complied without hesitation. But he wasn't alone today. He couldn't just leave Kara behind without a second thought. Dave looked at her quizzically now.

She knew what he was asking and had to admit, if only to herself, that she was pleasantly surprised at this unexpected act of thoughtfulness. He really wasn't such a bad guy after all.

"Go," she told him, her gesture reinforcing her words. "Don't worry about me."

Nodding, Dave climbed aboard and took a seat beside Kyle's distraught mother. When the ambulance doors closed, the last thing he saw was Kara, standing where he'd left her, watching the ambulance as it pulled away from the fairgrounds.

He had no idea why that struck him as so melancholy. With a shake of his head, he turned his attention to his patient.

It took a while to stabilize the boy and to stop the bleeding. When Kyle Taylor finally opened his eyes, several hours had passed. Dave had ordered a C.T. scan of his head to confirm that he'd sustained only a minor concussion and that there was no brain damage, minimal or otherwise. In between, he found himself reassuring the boy's mother and wishing that Kara was around. She seemed to be able to handle the woman better.

It wasn't exactly the way he'd intended on spending his day off. When he was finally finished, Dave walked out into the parking lot toward where he usually parked his car. And then he remembered. His car wasn't here. It was still parked at the fair.

At least, that was where he'd left it. Which was why

he was surprised to actually see it parked in the lot near the E.R. exit. And even more surprised to see Kara leaning against the hood like a model waiting for the photographer to get busy and earn his keep.

Curiosity had Dave picking up his pace as he crossed to his car. And her.

"What's up, Doc?" Kara grinned. "Sorry. I always wanted to say that." Straightening, she stood back from the vehicle. "I was beginning to give up hope that they'd ever let you out. The boy okay?" she asked.

"He's asking for ice cream and saying he wants to go back to the fair, so yes, he's okay. I'm not so sure about his mother. I'm keeping him overnight for observation. His mother's staying with him." He couldn't hold it back any longer. "What are you doing here?"

"Talking to you," she answered innocently, then said more seriously, "And I thought you might want your car. I was pretty sure they weren't going to bring you back in that ambulance."

"Good call." He frowned, still mystified. "I didn't give you the keys." As if to prove it to himself, he felt his pockets—and found the outline of his car keys.

"No," she agreed, "you didn't."

She knew what he was asking her, he thought, but he put it into words anyway. "Then how did you get the car here?"

The grin on her lips was pure mischief, he couldn't help noting. And damn if it wasn't getting to him. Bigtime.

"How to change the oil and jump-start a car weren't the only things my dad taught me," she told him, her eyes shining.

Chapter Ten

Dave would have been the first to admit that his memory of Kara's father was rather vague at this point, but he was pretty sure he remembered the man being easygoing and likable. Neil Calhoun hadn't struck him as the kind of man who would have passed on this sort of larcenous knowledge to his daughter.

"Your father taught you how to break into a car and hot-wire it?" he asked incredulously.

"That's all a matter of your point of view," she replied. "What my dad taught me was how to get into my car and start it if for some reason I lost my car keys and found myself stranded somewhere. As it happens, the procedure is pretty much the same for all standard cars."

He supposed her explanation sounded a bit more plausible, as well as in keeping with what he remembered of her father's character. But he was also having a little trouble accepting another piece of this puzzle that was Kara Calhoun.

"And you've been waiting here all this time for me to come out?" He found that really hard to believe, given how much they rubbed each other the wrong way.

"Had to," she told him innocently.

"You had to," he repeated incredulously. This he had to hear, Dave thought. "Why?"

"Because you're my ride home," she answered with a straight face. "A girl always goes home with the guy who brought her."

That sounded like something his mother would say. Or hers. Which brought him to another question.

"What about our mothers?" Because everything happened so abruptly, he'd left the park without letting his mother know he wouldn't be there to have lunch with her. It hadn't even occurred to him until now—and he knew his mother had a tendency to worry.

"I found them and let them know what happened— not that I had to," Kara told him. She saw him raise a quizzical eyebrow, debated stringing it out, then took pity on him and explained, "Story's already spreading around the fairgrounds. 'Local Doctor Saves Kid.' Our mothers put two and two together before I ever found them to say that you were off being super-doctor."

He supposed his stepping up as the situation occurred had ruined what she'd had in mind. But for someone who'd suffered a setback, she certainly looked pretty chipper about it.

"What about your great plan to teach them a lesson?" he asked.

Oddly enough, that was going perfectly. "Oh, as far as they're concerned, that's still moving forward," she assured him. "I told them I was coming to bring you your car and that I was going to wait for you until you finished taking care of the boy. Your mother wanted me to tell you that she's very proud of you."

Kara opened the car door on the passenger side, but instead of getting in, she asked him, "Are you hungry?"

Breakfast was a misty memory. He didn't even remember what he'd had. Then he'd been too busy with the boy from the fairgrounds to stop for lunch and now it was close to dinnertime. He saw no reason to pretend that he wasn't close to starving.

"I could eat," he allowed.

"Good." She bent over and reached into the passenger side. Straightening, she emerged with a foam container, the kind restaurant leftovers were usually packed in.

The instant he smelled food, his stomach began to cramp up, protesting its empty state. Nodding at the container, he asked her, "What's that?"

"Food," she answered simply. "I figured even heroes have to eat."

Opening the lid, he saw that she'd brought him one of those fast-food chain specialty burgers that were a limited-time offer. Currently out, this one threatened to disappear from the menu in the next thirty days. Somehow, that was supposed to make it more desirable to the consumer, and right now it was working.

"I'm not a hero," Dave told her, rejecting the label she'd just awarded him.

Kara smiled. He was surprised at how sunny that smile seemed. "You are to Kyle's mother."

Dave shrugged, unfazed. Turning sideways, he sat down in the passenger seat. As he bit into the cheeseburger, a look of sheer contentment came over his face.

Watching him, amused, Kara asked, "Tastes damn good, huh?"

As a doctor, he should know better. After all, this came under the heading of junk food, but right now he didn't care.

"When you're really hungry, there's nothing better," he confessed, taking another bite. For a second, he closed his eyes, relishing the taste.

Kara smiled, watching him eat for a moment. He really seemed to be enjoying that. She was glad she'd thought to stop and get him something.

"You know," she told him genially, "you're not as much of a dork as I thought you were."

She'd almost kept that to herself, thinking it might give him something to use against her, to poke fun at her. But then she told herself she couldn't go through life being paranoid, and besides, maybe it was time to hold out an olive branch to Dave. One of them had to be the bigger person and take the first step. And, after all, he *had* done a pretty selfless thing.

Dave slanted a glance toward her. "Thanks. I think."

"Hey, I don't mind giving credit where it's deserved," she told him. She had a hunch he'd be expecting a *little* of the "old" Kara to remain within the new, updated version. "Why don't you get in and I'll drive so you can finish eating your cheeseburger?" she suggested.

He was tempted, but it still didn't seem fair. "What about you? Aren't you hungry?"

"I ate waiting for you," she told him, which was partially true. Although she hadn't been hungry when she got his food, that changed as she waited. So she'd had a candy bar that she'd found at the bottom of her purse, vintage unknown. It was a wee bit stale. "Go on, get in," she coaxed. "Unless, of course, you're afraid to let me drive."

"Well, you got here in one piece without the keys. Which reminds me—take the keys." Digging into his pocket, Dave retrieved his car keys and held them out to her. "I'll feel better if you do it the conventional way."

"Spoilsport." She laughed. But she took the keys from him and got back in on the driver's side. She buckled up then waited for him to swing his legs inside the car and secure his seat belt. "Here, I'll hold your cheeseburger," she offered.

He surrendered the cheeseburger, placing it back into the box on top of the now-spilled French fries and handing that to her while he slid the metal tongue of his seat belt into place.

"Thanks," he told her, taking the meal back.

The slight movement of her shoulders in a careless shrug blended in with her verbal response. "Don't mention it."

"I mean for everything," he emphasized, his eyes holding hers. "Bringing the car, bringing food. I get caught up in a patient's care, and I tend to forget everything else," he confessed.

"Well, that's a good thing, isn't it? Aren't all doctors

supposed to be that selfless? Oh God," she groaned, as if suddenly becoming aware of something.

When she didn't follow it up with an attempt at an explanation, he looked at her. "Oh God what?" he prodded.

"I keep saying these good things about you. If I'm not careful, somebody overhearing us might think that we're actually friends," she told him flippantly.

He knew what she was doing. She was trying to make him think that she was still the old Kara with the flinty tongue. But she wasn't. She was caring despite her attempts to seem otherwise. His thoughts went to Gary that morning in the clinic. She had a good heart, as well. That went a long way to balancing things out in his book.

"Heaven forbid," he said, just before taking another bite of his cheeseburger.

"Yeah," she agreed, backing the car out of the parking space. "That's what I say."

She wove her way across the hospital grounds until she came to the exit. Within a few minutes, they were on the main thoroughfare, heading for the freeway.

Time for directions, she thought. "Okay, how do you want to do this?"

"Do what?" he asked.

She gave him his options. "Shall I drive to my place so you can drop me off and then drive yourself to your house, or do you want to stop by your place first and then take me to my apartment?"

The second choice seemed to be rather convoluted, but he kept that to himself. Instead, he said simply, "I pick option number one."

"You know, if you're not careful, you're going to have me thinking that you're actually a real person instead of this plaster saint I always believed that you were."

"Why on earth would you think I was a plaster saint?" he asked, completely mystified.

She looked at him, stunned. He didn't remember? It hardly seemed possible. She remembered perfectly. "Because that's the way you used to behave. As if you were holier than thou—or at least holier than me."

Was that it? Dave laughed quietly, shaking his head. "As I recall, it wouldn't exactly have taken much to be holier than you. You were hell on heels back then."

She was about to get slightly defensive of the girl she'd once been—the woman she still believed herself to be—but what he said next completely took the wind out of her sails.

"I really envied you that freedom."

Her eyes narrowed. "Freedom?" Kara echoed, a little confused.

"My father had certain expectations of his offspring," Dave confided.

Having made short work of his cheeseburger, he crumpled up the paper it had been wrapped in within the container and turned his attention to the French fries. They had long since ceased to be warm but they still tasted good. He couldn't remember when he'd last had fries. He allowed himself to savor the first one before continuing what he was saying.

"When you came right down to it, my dad expected me to be mature by the time I took my first step."

That didn't jibe with the man Kara remembered from those summer vacations.

"Your dad was a lovely man who was always a lot of fun," she protested, remembering the tall, robust man fondly.

Now that she thought about it, Dave looked a great deal like his late father. The same thick, dark hair, the same green eyes and broad shoulders. The only difference was that Dave's hair was a bit unruly while his father's had always appeared to be perfect.

"With you," Dave agreed readily. "Because you were a girl. Had I had a sister, I don't doubt he would have been more or less the same with her. I guess in his own way, he was a chauvinist," Dave theorized. "He didn't expect nearly as much from 'the softer sex,' as he liked to call them, as he did from the male of the species, namely me." He spared her a look. "I have no doubt that you and he would have probably gone a few rounds once you got older," he told her with certainty.

She felt for him. Your father was the parent you were supposed to bond with if you were a boy. How awful for Dave if his father had gotten so caught up in rigid expectations that there was no place for the more memorable moments. She had a boatload of the latter not just with her mother but with her father, as well.

She began to see Dave in a whole different light. "Was he hard on you?" she asked.

Was that pity in her voice? Or sympathy? Either way, it surprised him. He hadn't thought her capable of that sentiment, at least not where he was concerned. But then, he wouldn't have expected her to be thoughtful, either, and he was obviously wrong in that department.

In response to her question, he shrugged. "No more than was necessary, I suppose. He told me there were no do-overs in life and that I had to get it right the first time because the world had no patience for the losers and the inept." The corners of his mouth twisted in a mirthless smile. "God knew that he didn't," he added almost under his breath.

She thought how his relationship with his father had differed from hers with her own father. She worshipped the ground her father had walked on, and he had always made her feel secure in his love. She'd wanted to please her father, to reward him for his faith in her, but he'd never asked anything more of her than that she be a good person and that she be happy.

Because of him—and her mother—she was.

Kara took a breath. Dave probably didn't want to hear this, but she needed to say it anyway. "I'm sorry you had a rough time of it."

The French fry he'd just popped into his mouth went down the wrong way. He coughed, his eyes beginning to water. One hand on the wheel, Kara reached for her soda. Pulling it out of the cup holder, she held it up to him. He took it without offering a protest and drank deeply. The coughing subsided.

"Thanks," he said, finally catching his breath. And then he looked at her as he wiped away the dampness from the corners of his eyes. "You keep sounding like that and I'm going to ask to see some ID pretty soon. Either that or we need to swing by your mother's garage to check for a pod."

"Invasion of the Body Snatchers." She laughed. "Who *are* you and what have you done with Dave?

Talk about pod checking, I should be looking in *your* garage for one." And then she grinned. "You really are getting to be a revelation. I didn't picture you as someone who was a movie buff."

"I'm not," he told her honestly.

The hell he wasn't. "Then how do you explain all the movie references? The *accurate* movie references," she emphasized.

That was simple enough to explain. "I remember everything I read or see, even just in passing. And as for having a rough time of it—" he got back to her initial question "—I didn't. Living up to my father's high standards helped me achieve as much as I did. There are easier things than getting through medical school," he told her.

She was certain that it had been hard. But she was just as certain that he was capable of it. "You would have done that on your own. Don't look so surprised. Just because I gave you a hard time when we were kids doesn't mean I didn't think you were smart or capable of making something of yourself. Young as I was, I always *knew* you'd be somebody when you grew up. Truth was, you made me feel a little inadequate. That was part of the reason I gave you such a hard time," she confided.

"And what was the rest of the reason for giving me such a hard time? Why *did* you give me a such hard time, Kara?"

"I already told you," she answered, looking back at the road. Glancing at the speedometer, she realized that she was pressing down too hard on the gas. The needle was nosing its way past the sixty mark. She eased back.

The subject was getting her too agitated. *He* was getting her too agitated.

Dave did a quick mental review. No, he hadn't missed anything. "No, you didn't."

"Well, okay, maybe not in so many words," she allowed. Maybe the man didn't take behaving "holier than thou" as a reason to get her back up. "Because you looked down on me."

"No, I didn't," he protested. He'd thought of her as annoying, a brat and, at times, skillfully humiliating, especially for her age. But he'd never thought himself better than her. Just nicer.

She knew what she knew. "Yeah, you did. There was a two-year age difference between us, but it might as well have been twenty. Those two years made you act as if I were beneath you. Insignificant," Kara added for good measure, vividly remembering those years and how it felt.

Dave stuck to his guns. "That's not what I thought. You were so fearless, you made me feel self-conscious. And there was that incident with the snake," he reminded her pointedly. "You didn't exactly endear yourself to me with that."

Handling snakes had never bothered her. But she knew it bothered him and she'd acted on it. "That only happened later. After you—" She sighed, stopping herself. "Never mind, there's no point in rehashing all this old stuff. Just water under the bridge," she told him.

She didn't want to open up any old wounds and make them fresh. That could all be pushed into the background. She had a mother to ease into her place and so did he. That was far more important than renewing any old squabbles with him that she knew were not about to be won today.

Kara spared a glance in his direction. "Any fries left?"

He hadn't realized that he'd been eating all this time. The fries were almost all gone. But there were still a few stragglers left.

Dave raised his brow. "Want one?"

"No, I'm taking inventory," she answered sarcastically, then stopped herself. Maybe that sounded a little too sharp. She laughed a bit self-consciously. "Sorry, old habits die hard. Yes, I want one."

Since her hands were on the wheel, he decided just to put a French fry in her mouth. Taking the largest one that was left, he held it up to her lips and said, "I know I'm going to regret saying this, but open your mouth."

She turned her head slightly toward him. Even so, Dave saw that her eyes were laughing at him as she complied. When she closed her lips again, they brushed against his fingers.

Or perhaps his fingers brushed against her lips. In whatever order it happened, the effect was still the same. An electrical surge, quick and jolting, passed through both of them at the same time.

Chapter Eleven

Kara's skin felt hot and her heart suddenly leaped without warning, pounding madly like some impromptu marching-band drum soloist.

Belatedly, she shifted her eyes back to the road and realized she was about to go right through a red light. Alarmed, she slammed on the brakes.

Kara felt the back end of the vehicle fishtailing first to the right, then to the left as she attempted to compensate for the sickening lunge by turning the steering wheel quickly in the opposite direction.

The front tires had gone well over the intersection's white line before she finally managed to get the car to stop. Fortunately for them, there was no through traffic.

Her heart was pounding so hard that it hurt. She told herself it was because of the near miss, but it had begun beating erratically before she ever had to slam on her brakes and she knew it.

Her heart was pounding because of him. How dumb was that? she asked herself.

Beside her, Dave had both of his hands braced against the dashboard, anticipating a traumatic collision at the very least.

When there wasn't one, he blew out a breath and tried to relax. His neck and shoulders felt as stiff as if they'd suddenly been turned to iron.

"You charge extra for that?" he cracked, attempting to make light of the near-overwhelming moment.

Who *was* this man beside her? The Dave she remembered hadn't had a sense of humor—possibly because she hadn't really given him anything to laugh about, she thought now ruefully. But he would have definitely read her the riot act at being this careless—all but flying through a red light and then almost sending them both through the windshield in her attempt to stop the car.

Letting out a long, shaky breath, she shook her head in response to his question. "The first one's on the house," she told him.

Dave looked at the traffic light and then back at her. She wasn't moving.

"Light's green," he prompted and then leaned forward, peering closer at her. "And so are you," he observed.

"There's a reason for that," she murmured, moving her foot back to the gas pedal. Her stomach had tied itself up in a knot.

She wasn't used to doing stupid things like that. Granted, there were times when she drove fast, maybe a wee bit faster than the speed limit, but she was *never* reckless or preoccupied.

Until just this moment.

Once is all it takes, Kara reminded herself ruefully.

"You want to pull over for a minute?" Dave suggested. "We could switch places and I could take over. After all, it is my car and I've finished eating," he added.

She didn't want to surrender the driver's seat. If she did, she knew that she'd never hear the end of it from him. As it was, she probably wouldn't anyway, Kara thought.

Never hear the end of it? Listen to yourself, the little voice in her head silently mocked. *Like you're going to keep seeing him or running into him once this charade is over? C'mon, Kara. This is all temporary. You know that. What's wrong with you?*

She had no answer to that, no idea why she was behaving the way she was. She felt restless and unsettled, as if she was waiting for something to happen without really knowing what—or why.

"Kara, are you okay?" Dave was asking her. When she looked in his direction, she saw concern in his eyes.

"I'm fine," she snapped out a little too forcefully, ashamed of herself the moment she did. "Just can't seem to be able to eat and drive at the same time," she added a bit stiffly.

"Yeah, that must be it," he agreed for the sake of peace. But he didn't believe it for a second. Kara could easily do five things at once and keep track of each; she always had. Something else was going on here.

Most likely, he judged, the same "something" he'd felt himself.

"Sorry if I scared you," she said in a smaller voice that sounded completely unlike her usual one.

"Ditto."

It felt as if every single nerve she possessed had gone on red alert and no matter how she tried to talk herself out of it, they all refused to stand down.

She spared him a glance now and even though part of her understood what he was saying—that he'd sensed her reaction to him, to being fed by him—she asked sharply, "Excuse me?"

He knew that telling her to relax would only fall on deaf ears. Kara was the most contrary person he'd ever known, always ready to do the exact opposite of whatever she was told. The only way out of the situation— and an argument—was to make this about him, as well. It would keep this from escalating or becoming some kind of battle of wits, neither of which he wanted. And, he suspected, if really pressed for an honest answer, neither did she.

"I felt it, too," he told her quietly.

He might as well have shouted it. She could feel every vein in her body pulsing, making her grow extremely hot in the space of what felt like a nanosecond.

Still, being Kara, she felt compelled to deny the obvious. So she feigned ignorance. "Felt what?"

He wasn't exactly certain how to describe it. "That electrical spark," he finally said. "You know, when your lips brushed against my fingers."

Her back went up almost instantly. "You mean when *your* fingers brushed against *my* lips."

"Really?" he asked, his voice as quiet as hers was intense. "You're going to break this down into who did what to whom first? You really want to go that route?"

He didn't say it, but his tone indicated that she was being juvenile. And she supposed she was. But that was only because this reaction she'd just experienced—desire? Longing?—was very, very new to her. She supposed it was something that teens went through, but she'd never felt connected like this to anyone before, never felt herself growing hot with anticipation before. Imagined it, maybe, wondered about it, sure, but never actually experienced it. Not until just this moment.

"No," she answered with what she could only hope looked like a careless shrug. "Um, what was it that you think you felt?"

He knew exactly what she was doing. She wanted him to say it first. "I'll show you mine if you show me yours?" he guessed. With a laugh couched in disbelief, he shook his head. "Okay, I'll go first." He looked at her profile as they drove. Damn but it was near perfect, he thought. Why, after all this time, especially with their history, was she getting to him like this? "God help me, I felt something. And—" he took a breath, as if to fortify himself before continuing "—not for the first time."

Kara gripped the steering wheel harder. Her chin went up in unconscious defense. "This isn't my first time, either."

He realized that she'd misunderstood him. "I meant with you. Not my first time *with you*," he emphasized, trying to get his feelings across.

With her?

That completely threw her. Her eyes darted toward Dave quickly. Her heart decided to relocate back up into her throat, possibly permanently this time.

"Really?" Did that sound as breathless and tinny to him as it did to her? Her nerves were all over the place and she damned herself for it.

This is Dave, damn it. Nothing-special Dave. Don't act stupid.

"Really," Dave said. "Face it, Kara," he went on. "For whatever reason, there's an attraction between us."

She didn't want to face it. Didn't want to admit it or lower her defenses. She was actually *afraid* to lower her defenses. The only way to take the edge off this was to be flippant. So Dave would think that this was business as usual for her instead of completely uncharted territory.

"You probably have some kind of a scientific name for all this," Kara said.

Why in heaven's name would she think that? But then, the way her mind worked had always been a huge mystery to him and, he suspected, most likely to anyone else dealing with her.

"No," he told her simply.

He wasn't helping, Kara thought. If she wasn't careful, she'd find herself slipping into a vortex, one from which she didn't think she would ever emerge.

"Okay," she said gamely, "how about if we call it 'Albert'?"

It was official, he thought. He really hadn't a clue what went on in that head of hers. "'Albert'?" he questioned.

"Yes, Albert. As in Albert Einstein." Kara didn't

have to look at him to know that he was staring at her as if she'd lost her mind. Maybe she had, but this tiny tidbit actually did make sense. "According to one of the latest biographers, it seems that Albert Einstein had one heck of a raging libido."

That might or might not be true, he didn't know. But there was one thing he did know. "You're driving past your development," he told her.

Kara did a double take.

Damn it, he was right. She *was* driving past the entrance to her development. Pressing her lips together, she refrained from saying anything as she made her way to the next light that, fortunately, allowed for U-turns.

"I guess the conversation with you is so scintillating," she cracked dryly, "I didn't notice the entrance."

"I like you better without the sarcasm," Dave told her quietly.

Kara was grateful that they were inside his car so he couldn't tell she was blushing. Because of her fair skin, she was probably an embarrassing shade of pink right now.

Why his comment should do that to her was something she didn't completely grasp and refused to explore at the moment. The less she thought about him—or "them"—the better, she decided.

"I'll make a note of that when I get a chance," she promised flippantly.

"Right." He reminded himself that Kara *had* brought his car to him and that she had brought him something to eat, as well. She was under no obligation to do either, so beneath the bravado, there really was a very decent, kind person.

One who, for some unknown reason that pointed to the fact that God *had* to have a sense of humor, stirred him the way he really had never been stirred before.

Every single woman he had ever been out with—women he felt were close to perfect in temperament, women who'd matched his own personality and intellect—almost immediately left him restless, eager to be on his way. Bored. Every woman he thought he should be attracted to, he really wasn't.

And the one woman he would have bet his soul that he *wasn't* attracted to, he was. How was that for a cosmic joke at his expense? Dave thought darkly.

Kara drove into her development, but rather than take the first available space in guest parking, she continued driving until she came to a second set of guest parking spaces. He hadn't even noticed them when he came to pick her up.

She finally picked a space, parking in the last empty one that was closest to her apartment.

"Less distance to walk," she explained when she saw him looking at her quizzically.

Taking a breath, as if bracing herself, Kara unbuckled her seat belt and opened the driver's-side door, then got out.

Dave quickly followed suit on his side, emerging from the vehicle at the same time she did.

Time to beat a hasty retreat, she thought nervously, feeling disgusted with herself at the same time for her reaction. Just what was it that she was afraid of? She'd always been so fearless around Dave, had always enjoyed being able to tease him. Since when did she subscribe to the better-safe-than-sorry school of thought? And exactly what was she being "safe" from?

Still, she heard herself saying, "Well, I'll give you a call when I figure out the next phase of Operation Meddling Mothers."

To her surprise, rather than agree or just say goodbye the way she expected him to, Dave looked at her over the hood of his car and said, "The world won't end if you invite me in, you know."

Stunned, she was certain she hadn't heard him correctly. And if she had, then he needed to explain why he'd just said what he had. "What?"

His eyes held hers as he began to repeat his statement. "The world won't—"

"No, I heard you. I heard you," she cried, holding up her hand to stop him from going on. "And you're wrong," she told him. There went her pulse again. What was *wrong* with her, anyway? "It just might. Why throw the whole universe off just to continue with an experiment named Albert—?"

It was the last thing she said.

Dave had rounded the back of his car while she was talking and, right when she'd started to voice her last question, he'd framed her face with his hands, drew her to him and kissed her.

He kissed her not as if it were some sort of an experiment, but as if he'd been restraining himself from reaching over while they were still on the road and kissing her right then and there.

There was enough energy and passion within the kiss to completely take her breath away—as well as, in her opinion, to supply enough electricity to light up Las Vegas for a week.

Part of her, for just a split second, wanted to flee. To run and save herself before it was too late. But that survival instinct died quickly. Survival was the last thing on her mind. Enjoyment coupled with eagerness and excitement took center stage, wiping everything else from her brain cells.

Her knees went weak, as did the pit of her stomach. To steady herself—or perhaps to anchor Dave into place—she put her arms around his neck, holding him closer to her. Savoring the taste of him as her head continued to spin madly around.

He wanted her too much.

The way Dave saw it, while he was still capable of coherent thought, was that he had one of two options. He could either run like hell and find himself fighting off this urge time and again, even when she wasn't anywhere around. Perpetually wondering if he was missing out on something.

Or, he could just follow his instincts, make love with this one-time harpy from his past and most likely discover that the expectations ricocheting through him right now were far too high. Then, once again, he would find himself being greatly disappointed in the person he'd selected because she wasn't what he'd hoped she was—someone who actually made him feel alive and grateful to be so.

Still, he couldn't very well force himself on Kara. She needed to make her own choice.

Drawing back, Dave looked at her. He pulled in a

somewhat ragged breath before he asked, "So, are you going to invite me in?"

Shell-shocked, Kara looked around, more than half expecting that civilization as she knew it had self-destructed.

Apparently, it hadn't. She had no idea why everything was still intact. God knew she wasn't.

"You mean you're not in yet?" she murmured, her voice low and husky.

She looked so dazed. Dave bit his lower lip to keep from laughing at the confusion in her eyes. There was almost something endearingly sweet about her expression, even though he knew better than to comment on that or point it out to her. If he did, it would probably be the last thing he'd get to say on this earth.

So instead, he gave her a serious answer and said, "No, not yet. We're still standing out here in guest parking."

"Not for long," she assured him. Taking his hand in hers, she pulled him along in her wake. Looking over her shoulder, she told him, "I have no intentions of remaining in 'Park' any longer than I really have to."

Ignoring the warmth that anticipation was spreading through his limbs—hadn't he been disappointed enough times to know that this was all eventually leading nowhere?—Dave laughed.

"You never struck me as someone who could keep from moving around for long."

She looked at him over her shoulder again as she dug through her purse, searching for her keys. "I guess we're about to find out a lot of things, aren't we?"

Yes, he thought, *I guess we are.*

Chapter Twelve

As he walked across the threshold into Kara's apartment, Dave waited for his common sense to prevail. At that moment, he had every intention of stalling, of giving them both time to think through what seemed to be on the verge of happening.

Those were his intentions.

But then Kara turned around and looked at him with those incredible blue eyes of hers. And just like that, all the air around him evaporated, making it almost impossible for him to catch his breath.

Impossible to do anything but focus on her and this sudden, intense and overwhelming need he felt raging inside of him.

What the hell was going on with him anyway?

This wasn't him, he argued. He wasn't given to feeling these kinds of passions and desires. He was far more sedate than that.

Yet here he was, his mouth sealed to hers, his body heated in anticipation of what was to come.

Maybe if she hadn't kissed him back the way she had, his ardor might have dampened slightly and his mind would have been able to prevail, to take control. But the moment they came together, Dave could feel her responding to him, could taste the desire on her lips. In less time than it took to draw in a breath, all bets were off and sanity went straight out the window.

Dave was only vaguely aware of moving into Kara's living room, but he was acutely aware of her. The way her curves fit into the spaces of his body. The way her skin felt like the softest newly spun silk. And the way her mouth worked over his, fueling his passion and moving it up to the next level. Had he been a lit torch instead of a man, he would have burned so brightly that no one within miles could miss it.

His downfall, he knew, was inevitable.

Kara was in trouble and she knew it. This was no longer pretending, going through the motions for the benefit of their mothers. *This* was something that was happening in the privacy of her apartment with no one to see what was going on but the two of them. There was no excuse for this, no reason for it to be happening.

None except that she was going to self-destruct if it didn't. If he didn't make love to her soon and thus uncork the volatile forces that threatened to implode her if they weren't released, she was certain her minutes were numbered.

Survival meant only one thing. She needed to make love with this man.

Now.

With her hands amazingly a great deal more steady than what was going on inside of her, Kara began to peel Dave's T-shirt away from his rock-hard chest. She dragged it up over his head and threw it on the floor without missing a beat. Her lips were hardly separated from his.

When she began to uncinch his belt, Dave reached behind her, found the knot holding together her halter and started to untie it. For a second, she felt him fumbling as the knot initially gave him trouble, but finally the ties fluttered apart, one to either side of her, leaving her exposed.

She could have sworn she felt a hot breeze pass over her bare skin as she anticipated what was to come next.

She felt him catch his breath as his hands passed over her breasts lightly, reverently, as if she were breakable and required the utmost care.

Her heart began to hammer so hard, Kara was certain it was going to crack a rib.

She didn't care. It was worth it.

Reacting to the way his fingers caressed her, she kissed him harder. His touch was gentle, soft, but there was no question. At this singular moment in time, Dave owned her. She was his without a word needing to be uttered.

Kara drew in a fortifying breath, then began undressing him again. With less-than-certain moves, she pushed his jeans down over his hips. The moment he was left wearing only his underwear, it was as if Dave suddenly snapped to attention and got busy. Within the next two heartbeats, she was no longer in her denim short-shorts. One more heartbeat and the white thong she'd had on beneath them became history, as well.

A slight groan escaped her lips. Trying her best to keep her wits about her, Kara returned the compliment in kind. She hooked her thumbs beneath each side of his underwear and pulled it down with one quick snap of her wrists.

Their bodies hot, their desire hotter, they came together like the opposite fields of a magnet, sealed against one another, their mouths still questing, still devouring.

And then she was on the floor with Dave's body over hers.

Breaking contact, his mouth moved from hers. But there was no respite in the offing. His lips were already moving along the sensitive side of her neck, driving her absolutely crazy as desires she'd never felt before suddenly came to life within her core. Kara arched her body into his, trying to capture this sensation he was creating inside her.

As his mouth slid down, bringing havoc to everywhere his lips and tongue touched, it stoked an urgency within her that was threatening to explode. Kara found herself in the throes of a sweet agony she'd never even suspected could exist.

And then stars exploded as his tongue found what was to her a brand-new pressure point. Next to no extra contact was required before bursting rockets joined the stars, obliterating her sky, utterly and completely disorienting her.

As she fell back, gasping, her eyes reduced to small slits, she could still make out his expression. Dave wasn't smug, but there was a smile curving his mouth. A definite smile that denoted triumph.

Seeing it caused her to rally, to somehow find a second wind and to silently vow that she was not the only one who was going to undergo this kind of wondrous torture.

With a quick movement, she caught him off guard and managed to flip their positions. Within a blink of an eye, she was over him.

Taking her time, teasing, moving forward and then back, she swept the tip of her tongue over him. With that one weapon, she successfully brought him to the brink, only to retreat again.

Once.

Twice.

As she ventured toward a third time, Dave caught her wrists, tugged her over to one side and was on top of her again. No more games, he thought. He could only hold himself in check for so long before it all slipped beyond his control.

His eyes on hers, vaguely mystified how he and the person he'd thought of as his mortal enemy close to twenty years ago had gotten to this place, he brought his mouth down on hers. Completely lost in her, he kissed her over and over again until they were both in danger of simply dissolving in a puff of steam.

Parting her legs with his knee, the warmth of her core guiding him, Dave began to enter her slowly.

And then stopped.

His eyes widened and he looked at her, dumbfounded.

He saw her looking back at him, something almost defiant in her crystal-blue orbs.

Drawing back, he managed to form the words, "Are you—?"

She threw the word "yes" back at him, thrust her hips upward and the discussion-that-wasn't became a moot point.

They were one now.

Her hips moved in tandem with his, initially setting a pace until he took over. And then she mimicked him, not just echoing his movements but actually anticipating them. It seemed almost impossible for him to believe that this was their first time, they were that in sync.

And yet, it was. It was their first time together.

And it was hers, as well.

His arms tightened around her protectively as the last moment seized him, bringing him to the mind-numbing, heart-pounding climax he sought. For a frozen moment in time, it held on to him as tightly as he held on to her. And then, the effects began to loosen, to recede, until he was left with a semi-racing pulse and encroaching confusion mingled with guilt.

The euphoria disappeared.

The guilt didn't.

Shifting, he dropped down rather than simply lay down beside her, his heart rate slowly returning to normal.

"You're a virgin," he said hoarsely.

"Not anymore," she corrected, a wide, satisfied grin on her lips.

He was completely mystified. Gathering together

what little strength he had left, Dave propped himself up on one elbow and fixed her with an unwavering gaze, trying to sort things out. And failing miserably.

"How is that possible?" he wanted to know.

"Well, you see," she began calmly, "when little girls are born…"

Holding on to his temper, Dave let out an impatient breath. "I know how it's possible," he bit off. "I'm asking you how the hell you got to be one."

"I'm trying to tell you," she answered innocently, "I started out that way."

Damn it, she knew what he meant, he insisted silently. It didn't make any sense to him. "But you're thirty."

"Nothing gets by you."

"You might have a disposition like a viper, but you *are* beautiful. There had to be all sorts of guys who could put up with that tongue of yours for a little while," he theorized, then came to the crux of his question. "How the hell did you stay a virgin?"

"Clean living?" she offered, widening her eyes innocently.

He was really losing his temper now. She was jerking him around, the way she used to when they were forced to spend their summers together. The memories it brought back were far from sweet.

"Damn it, Kara," he snapped. "I'm dealing with monumental guilt here. The least you can do is give me a serious answer to my question."

In all the ways she'd pictured him, she'd never envisioned him feeling guilty. It made him seem all too human to her. She felt something beginning to stir inside. Again.

"There's nothing to feel guilty about," she assured him calmly. "In case you didn't notice, this wasn't exactly one-sided." She punctuated her statement with another wide grin.

Dave let out a ragged breath, then slowly took one in, trying his best to center himself. He didn't believe in things like Zen, but he knew the merit of breathing correctly. And slowly.

It helped. A little.

Okay, he was going to ask one more time. He *needed* to know and he wanted a straight answer from her. "Why didn't you ever sleep with anyone before now?"

Her eyes danced with humor as she looked at him. "If this is what you call *sleeping,* you must be hell on wheels when you're awake."

Okay, he'd had enough. He'd tried but there was just no winning with this woman. "Damn it, Kara—"

She held up one hand, the other holding the blanket she'd had across the back of the sofa that was now pressed against her. "Okay, okay, you want an answer, I'll give you an answer. Because I decided long ago that I wasn't going to do it just to do it."

Her decision, she didn't tell him, had been arrived at shortly after her father had died. Shortly after her mother's heart had been broken into so many pieces she'd been afraid it would *never* work right again. It was also at that time when she'd sworn off getting serious with the male of the species. Ever. And she'd kept her word. Until just now.

"That the only way I was ever going to wind up

naked and spread-eagle with a guy was if my emotions were engaged. So far, they never had been." She saw the alerted expression on his face and laughed shortly. Just as she'd thought. "Oh, don't look like Bambi caught in the headlights. Relax, you don't have anything to worry about. I figured it was high time for me to finally do it, so I decided to do it with someone I'd known forever." It was a desperate lie, but, she judged, a believable one. "You happened to fall into that category, that's all. It's that simple. Scout's honor," she added, forming what she hoped was the scout pledge salute.

Well, it sure as hell didn't feel simple, not to him, Dave thought. Maybe he was old-fashioned, but he still believed that a girl's first time was supposed to be something she would remember forever, not something that happened on the spur of the moment on the floor of her apartment.

"You should have let me know," he insisted, his voice accusing.

"I would have, but I must have misplaced my business cards. It's printed right under my name," she told him, her face deadly serious. "'Kara Calhoun, Resident Virgin. Approach at your own risk,'" she concluded with a wicked grin.

"Can you stop being flippant for one damn minute? Do you think you can do that for me?" he demanded.

Where did he get off talking to her like that? she thought, annoyed. "I'm not sure. I can try," she said, acting as if she were as dumb as a proverbial post.

Dave surprised her by looking at her seriously. "Are you all right with this?" he wanted to know. "I mean…"

She put her finger to his lips, knowing that he could

probably go on and on and say nothing and still feel tortured while he was doing it.

"I know what you mean," she assured him, "and I think it's actually kind of sweet. Yes," she told him in reply, "I'm all right with this. I would have told you to stop if I'd wanted you to, or if I had a change of heart. That's *why* it was all right."

He shook his head, slipping his arm back around her and lying down again. "You know I'm never going to understand you."

She grinned. "Luckily for you, you don't have to. Hey, since you broke me in—"

"Oh God," he groaned, hating the way that sounded. How could she be so cavalier about something so intimate as making love?

"Can we do it again?" she continued, looking at him to gauge his response. "I mean, it was nice and— Oh, unless you can't do it again," she said suddenly, realizing she might be asking for more than he could deliver at the moment. "I heard that some guys can only do it once, and then they need to recharge. Kind of like a cell phone that loses all its power after a series of calls."

He rose on his elbow again to look at her. Dave shook his head. Damn but he should run for the hills before he slipped any further into this field of quicksand he'd wandered into.

He felt it was a dangerous sign that he really didn't want to flee. That he wasn't at least *trying* to make a run for it. But he didn't want to. He wanted to be exactly where he was. Here, with her. About to make love with her all over again.

"You're insane," he told her, peering at her face. "You know that, right?"

"So you keep telling me," she said with a sigh. "So I take it that's a no?"

Curious as to how her brain actually worked, he asked, "Why would you think that would automatically be a no?"

"Because—" She stopped suddenly, her eyes widening in surprise. And then pleasure. Dave was leaning against her, his still very naked, very rugged body touching hers. In all the right places. Grinning wickedly, she laughed. "Oh, wait, maybe you *do* want to do it again."

The woman would have been downright embarrassing if he wasn't mercifully past that point with her. "Kara?"

Settling in against him, anticipation humming through her veins, she turned her face up to his. "What?" she asked, her voice almost melodic.

The order was short and to the point. "Shut up."

She grinned. Dave was so predictable. In an odd sort of way, she found that comforting. "Okay, I can do that."

"I sincerely doubt it," he replied.

There was no such thing as true silence with Kara, only less talking. And then, to keep her from saying another word, he did the only thing he could. He effectively sealed his mouth to hers.

And with that, they began the sultry, stimulating dance all over again.

Chapter Thirteen

Sleep slowly peeled away from Kara's brain one layer at a time.

When she finally opened her eyes to the intrusive early-dawn light, she discovered that she was curled up against Dave with her arm splayed possessively across his chest.

Startled, shaken, she nearly bolted upright and pulled her arm away. At the last minute, she managed to stop herself.

Kara slowly exhaled a sigh of relief. She was certain that the sudden movement would have woken Dave up, and she wasn't ready for that yet. She had no idea what to say. She'd never had a "morning after" conversation, mainly because she'd never had a "morning after"—or "a night before" for that matter.

And even if she'd had one of those nights in her past,

it definitely wouldn't have prepared her for this, for waking up and finding herself next to Dave, still apparently as naked as the day she was born.

And so, from what she could detect, was he.

What the hell had she been thinking? How in heaven's name had she allowed this whole situation to get so far out of control?

She knew the story that she'd given Dave, one she'd made up on the spur of the moment, but it had been a lie. She had no overwhelming desire to join the huge ranks of the nonvirgins. Old-fashioned though it might sound, she actually—until last night—had felt that lovemaking was supposed to happen with someone who meant something to her. With someone who meant *everything* to her, not someone with whom she engaged in frequent verbal sparring matches.

Damn it, what *had* she been thinking? Or, more to the point, *why* hadn't she been thinking? What was it about her childhood arch enemy, her irritating-as-hell adolescent nemesis, that turned her into an eager participant in the lovemaking game?

And why the hell was she smiling like the Cheshire cat?

Despite her mental upbraiding, Kara could still feel her lips curving. Amid the nerve endings that were standing at attention, all on high alert, she could feel an unaccountable surge of, well, *happiness* for lack of a better word.

Damn it, she didn't want to be happy about this, *couldn't* be happy about this. She and Dave didn't have a relationship, not the kind that didn't require sharpened tongues at ten paces, at any rate. There was no future in this—not a single chance in hell. It would be like allowing herself to fall in love with a fictional character, someone like Shakespeare's Romeo.

No, not Romeo, she amended. There was no way anyone would ever mistake the very precise, exceedingly straitlaced and orderly Dr. Dave Scarlatti for the impetuously passionate character Shakespeare had penned. If she had to compare him to a fictional character, Dave was more like the stern, honorable Atticus Finch from *To Kill A Mockingbird,* more prone to loving principles than a flesh-and-blood woman.

No, not him, either, she thought in the next moment, rejecting that image. God, but she felt confused.

There was a headache growing between her eyes.

"A penny for your thoughts."

Her heart slammed into her rib cage at the sound of his voice. Kara clamped her lips together to keep from uttering a gasp. She'd thought he was still asleep.

Recovering, she took a breath to steady her nerves. "Sorry, at this point my thoughts are up to at least five-fifty."

"Five-fifty? Inflation's a bear," he commented with a laugh. He studied her face for a moment, making a judgment call. "Okay, I'm good for it. What are you thinking about?"

There was no time to be creative, or even make up a last-minute lie. That left her no choice but to go with the truth, odd though it might sound. "What fictional character you're most like."

"And?" he asked. "What conclusion did you come to?" *This should be interesting,* he couldn't help thinking, bracing himself.

She shrugged, her blond hair brushing along her bare shoulder. "I can't come up with anyone."

"That means I'm either very unique, or so nondescript I don't even leave an impression," he theorized, amused. His eyes on hers, he asked, "Which is it?"

She sighed again. Why did he scramble her insides this way? Why, with all the men she interacted with— her field was still dominated by mostly males of all ages—did *he* turn out to be the one who lit her fire?

"I'll let you know when I figure it out. So, until then—"

She was about to wiggle her way out of bed, taking the blanket with her to cover up, when her phone rang. Now what?

Nobody ever called her at this hour in the morning, not if they didn't want their head taken off. They knew better.

Kara was tempted not to answer it, but one glance at caller ID told her that her mother was on the other end. She had a better chance of growing six inches in the next half hour than she did of avoiding her mother. There was no escaping the woman. Paulette Calhoun would just keep calling and calling all day long, not leaving any messages, until the receiver was finally picked up.

Better to face the music now than listen to the intro all day long, anticipating some kind of dire repercussions, coming up with scenarios in her head that were probably way off.

Exhaling loudly, she silently counted to ten and then yanked the receiver off its cradle, pressing it against her ear. "Good morning, Mother. My, you're up early," she noted with sarcasm.

"Couldn't sleep," her mother confessed, as if imparting some sort of dark secret.

Tell me about it. Kara could remember being grilled by her mother as a teenager—where she went, who she went with, all the typical mother questions. These days she understood better why her mother had done it, but at the time, it seemed like a huge invasion of privacy.

Right now, of course, it still was.

"They have pills for that, Mother. Pop two and sleep until morning," she recommended cheerfully.

Since her daughter wasn't asking her what was keeping her up, Paulette volunteered the information. "I kept thinking about you and Dave."

Kara's eyes narrowed. There wasn't even an attempt at subtlety on her mother's part. "They have pills for that, too. You can find them in the reality section of your local pharmacy."

It was obvious to Kara that her mother had no intentions of allowing herself to be drawn into a verbal sparring match. "Did you bring Dave's car to him?"

Here came the headache, full force, Kara thought. "That I did."

"And?" Her mother made no attempt to hide the eagerness in her voice.

"And he took it, just as you might have suspected, Mother." What did the woman want from her? A blow-by-blow statement written in blood?

She could almost see her mother shaking her head. "How did you ever get so sarcastic?"

"It's a gift," Kara quipped. "Did you call for something specific, Mother? Or just to harass me in general?"

"I just wanted to know if you saw Dave last night after you took off from the fair, that's all," her mother answered.

"I gave him his car, so I pretty much would have had to see him, now, wouldn't I, Mother?" Out of the corner of her eye, she could see Dave taking this all in. And grinning, damn him.

"If you gave him the car, how did you get home, dear?" her mother asked innocently.

She was fishing, Kara thought. And being painfully obvious about it. "He drove me, Mother."

"And let you off at your door?" her mother guessed innocently.

It was official. The headache had exploded all over her forehead. "Instead of playing twenty questions, Mom, why don't you just invest in a surveillance camera so you can have all your questions answered before you even have to ask them."

Her mother absolutely refused to get angry and hang up. "Then what would we have to talk about?" she asked innocently.

"Normal things," Kara shot back.

"Asking about my daughter's social life *is* a normal thing, dear," her mother pointed out. "At least, it is to everyone but you."

Completely distracted by her mother, Kara wasn't prepared to suddenly feel Dave's hand brush up against her inner thigh and *definitely* wasn't prepared to feel that immediate, intense reaction to him that was now ripping through her like a tornado. She let out a gasp.

"Did you just yelp?" Paulette asked, picking up on the sudden sound.

Kara swallowed a curse. That was a dirty trick, she thought angrily.

"No," Kara denied with feeling, batting away Dave's hand and glaring at him. What had gotten into him? "No, I didn't yelp. Must be something wrong with the connection."

She didn't like the long, drawn-out pause on the other end of the line. She could only surmise that her mother must be thinking, and that was never a good thing. Her mother possessed far too fertile an imagination.

"Kara, is he there with you right now?" her mother asked suddenly.

She was right. This wasn't good. Rather than just wasting her breath with a denial, Kara turned the tables and asked *her* a question. "What makes you think that, Mother?"

The answer came with no hesitation. "Because I can hear him breathing."

That was absurd. Kara couldn't even hear him breathing. She could, however, much to her downfall, *feel* him breathing, because his breath was trailing along her neck and upper torso and swiftly undoing her.

"No, you can't," Kara insisted.

"Aha, so he *is* there." Her mother sounded imminently pleased with herself. Too late Kara realized that she'd fallen for the trap. "Give him the phone, Kara."

Kara blew out an annoyed breath, knowing it was utterly useless to argue with her mother. So far, the woman was winning all the points.

"Here," she muttered, holding out the receiver to Dave. "My mother wants to talk to you."

If he was surprised, he didn't show it. Dave took the phone from her and put it to his ear. "Hello, Mrs. Calhoun, how are you?"

Kara closed her eyes. This whole scenario was just too bizarre for words.

"I'm fine, Dave, thank you. Tell me, how did that little emergency of yours go yesterday? Is the little boy all right?"

Dave was surprised at the show of concern. But then, as he recalled, Kara's mother had always been a very caring person. As had her father. "He's fine, thanks for asking."

And then Paulette Calhoun got down to business. "Listen, Dave, would you and my daughter be free for dinner next Saturday, say about six?"

"Let me find out," he told her. Cradling the receiver against his ear, he asked Kara, "Are you free next Saturday for dinner at six?"

Other than work, she had no set schedule, and as far as she knew, there was no overtime in her immediate future. But the invitation wasn't coming from him, it was coming from her mother.

This is all supposed to be part of your plan, dummy. Why is there this enormous pit in the middle of your stomach?

Maybe it had something to do with making wild, passionate love all over her apartment, culminating in her bedroom, and then waking up to find Dave in her bed—the very last place she would have *ever* rationally thought to find him. But then last night hadn't been very rational, had it?

She shrugged, and the blanket she had wrapped around her torso sank a little. She tugged it back into place. "I guess so."

Putting the receiver back up against his ear, Dave told her mother, "Kara says yes."

"Wonderful," Paulette cried with enthusiasm. "Then I'll see you both here next Saturday at six. Oh, by the way, you've probably already surmised this, but your mother will be here, as well. We're having a few friends over. Tell my daughter to wear something sensible."

Kara overheard that and the directive struck a nerve. She felt compelled to call out, "I'm coming in a bikini, Mother."

Paulette sighed audibly. "As long as all the important places are covered, dear, I suppose it's all right." And then she added, "Good luck, Dave."

He didn't bother to try to stifle the laugh that came to his lips. "Thank you, Mrs. Calhoun. I think I'll need it. We'll see you and my mother next week."

Deliberately leaning over Kara, he reached over to the nightstand and hung up the phone. As he drew back again, his chest brushed against hers. "Are you hungry?" he asked as if a jolt of electricity hadn't just traveled between them.

"Yes." But she wasn't as hungry for food as she was for something else.

Was this normal? she couldn't help wondering. After all, they wound up making love a total of three times last night. Any curiosity about the act of lovemaking and the sensations that were involved with it should have all been laid to rest by now, not wildly stirred up the way they felt right at this moment. But that, she knew, was because his body, naked beneath that section of sheet he had over his hips, had come in contact with her equally naked body.

It would help, she upbraided herself sternly, if she stopped fantasizing about him.

Something in her voice caught his attention and he gave up the idea of getting out of bed and cooking, at least for the moment. Still, he kept up the pretense—wasn't that what this was all ultimately about? Pretending?

Or maybe, he amended, in light of things that seemed to be happening, about pretending to pretend?

His eyes delved into hers. "What are you in the mood for?" he asked.

Kara had to suppress a groan. Oh God, he'd fed her such a straight line. It took everything she had not to give voice to the answer that had instantly sprung to her lips: *You.*

Instead, with effort, she told him, "Surprise me."

"Tall order," he commented, his eyes slowly caressing her face.

Even first thing in the morning, Kara was still beautiful. Maybe, Dave amended, even *more* beautiful than she'd been last night.

Just his luck, he thought with an inward sigh. He was falling for her. All the intelligent, poised, even-tempered, clear-thinking women in the world and *he* had to fall for the one emotional, volatile, outspoken harpy in the lot.

"Oh, you're up to it," she replied with confidence,

her voice so low it felt as if it were rumbling along his naked skin.

This was where he got up and marched off to the kitchen, dressed in confidence if nothing else, he told himself, because what was unfolding between them was way too hot to indulge in.

This was where he got up from the bed and put some distance between them.

Quickly.

This was where he—

Oh damn, he knew exactly where "this" was all leading him: to hell in a handbasket.

In one swift movement, he went from being next to her to looming directly over her. Bracketing her face with his hands, he paused for a moment, looking at her as if he'd never seen her before. And maybe he hadn't, at least, not *this* version of Kara, the one who seemed to so effortlessly fire up his soul.

He finally gave voice to what he was thinking. "You just might single-handedly set the course of cosmetics back half a century."

She wasn't altogether sure she understood where he was going with this.

"And why is that?" she wanted to know, waiting for a punch line she could rip apart. Secretly *hoping* for a put-down so that this feeling inside of her, this caramel center, melting feeling would finally go away instead of undoing her.

"Because you're beautiful without it. *More* beautiful without it," he corrected himself.

Still ready and waiting to read him the riot act, Kara came to a skidding halt before she was able to utter a single word. As his words sank in, she looked at him, utterly stunned and speechless. And confused.

What the hell was he up to? Was this some kind of bait and switch?

Mentally, she threw up her hands as his began to roam over her body, discovering her pressure points all over again.

"You don't play fair," she accused, the words scraping out of her dry mouth. The rest of her, however, was all but salivating with anticipation.

"Maybe," he told her slowly, his warm breath creating havoc everywhere it touched, "that's because I'm not playing at all."

Okay, now he really had her confused. "What are you saying?" she asked with effort, unable to draw in a complete sustaining breath.

"You're a bright woman," he told her, his lips beginning to unravel her again as they proceeded to tease all the different parts of her body. "You can figure it out."

Maybe she could. But that was for later.

Much later, she told herself, slipping her arms around Dave's neck. She planned to be far too busy right now to think at all.

Chapter Fourteen

This was crazy, Dave thought.

It was nearly a month later, and rather than winding down, the way both he—and, he was certain, Kara—had expected, things were only becoming more intense, more complex and, consequently, more confusing.

He knew he sure as hell was confused by this unexpected turn his life had taken. A month ago, he would have never seen this coming. And yet, here it was, confounding him even as it mocked him.

Damn it all, anyway.

It didn't make any sense to him. The only woman he'd ever actually felt as if he'd made a connection with was the one woman he never thought he'd *want* to make a connection with.

Somewhere in the universe, something was either seriously off-kilter, or God had the kind of twisted sense of humor none of the nuns ever publicized in the parochial school he'd attended.

And the really weird thing about all of this was that the further away their "breakup" was pushed back—as it had been twice already—the more he secretly found himself *wanting* to have it pushed back.

Something else he would have never expected.

It was as if he was in on the planning of his own self-destruction.

And he was *smiling* about it, Dave thought darkly, catching a glimpse of himself in the shiny surface of a stainless-steel cabinet door in the tiny room where he kept all the free clinic's medications locked up.

He thought back to the beginning, which now seemed like eons ago. Back then, this charade of falling for one another was to last only a week. Ten days, tops. Kara was supposed to have picked a fight with him at her mother's house the first Saturday they had been invited over for diner.

That had fallen through by mutual consent when Paulette Calhoun surprised them by inviting a few other people to dinner, as well. People, as it turned out, who came equipped with deep pockets and even deeper hearts. Over dinner Kara's mother had talked up the free clinic where he volunteered, praising all the good it was doing for the destitute people in that neighborhood.

Conversationally, she let it drop that the clinic was facing a funding shortage and she lamented the possibility that it might have to close its doors. She added that it would be morally criminal if that did happen, because all the children in that neighborhood would have nowhere to go if they became ill. Her guests, parents all, could readily identify with the angst of parents who had to stand by and watch their children suffer.

There was no question about it. The woman was good. He began to see where Kara got her craftiness and her stubbornness.

He vividly remembered how surprised—and, damn it, how relieved—he was that evening when Kara had drawn him aside and said in a hushed voice, "We can't get into a fight in front of these people now. They might think you're unstable and change their minds about those checks they've promised to send you for the clinic."

He'd wanted to point out that since she was the one who was to start the argument, most likely her mother's guests would think *she* was the unstable one. But he bit his tongue and merely nodded.

And just like that, there was a stay of execution. A stay that per force wound up extending his time in purgatory—or hell, depending on the point of view. Except that, even though he told himself that was what pretending to be romantically involved with Kara was supposed to feel like, being forced to spend time with her, presumably where her mother or his would be able to cross their paths, didn't feel like either hell or purgatory to him.

What he *did* feel like was, well, *alive*. Whether it was his anger that she periodically managed to arouse, or something else, there was no denying that the bottom line was that she did arouse him.

Very much so.

And even when he wasn't around her, she was haunting his thoughts as well as his dreams. There seemed to be no getting away from Kara. His head was utterly filled with visions of her that popped into his brain unprovoked, unannounced and utterly unbidden.

The woman had definitely cast some kind of spell over him, and while he didn't actually believe in things like voodoo, *something* had to be at play here that wasn't readily explainable.

Why else would he be thinking of her so much? Why else would he be looking forward to getting together with her, even if it was just to argue, the way they seemed to do about half the time that they were together? There was no denying that she was an infuriating, utterly perverse person.

The other half of the time, he'd already noted more than once, somehow managed to find them winding up in bed, whether it was after coming home from dinner at her mother's, or after a quick visit to his mother's place, or just after a long, hard day's work.

The charade—and their lovemaking—had fallen into almost a pattern. Chaotic, but nonetheless still a pattern.

When he felt dead tired after a day in the E.R., she would turn up in the parking lot, waiting for him, the scent of a hot pizza emanating from inside her car. And the times that his shift actually ended on a quiet note and *she* had put in copious amounts of overtime on some kind of save-the-world video game that was overdue for production, he'd invite her to his place, where he proceeded to whip up something seductively appetizing to romance her mouth. And then he'd proceed, after dinner, to do the same to the rest of her. It all seemed to follow so naturally.

In short, he thought as he made some quick notations to the file of the patient he'd just seen, he was enjoying himself. For the first time in his life, there was something beyond his work that he found himself looking forward to.

Even arguing with the woman was enjoyable, because somewhere amid the words that threatened to grow more and more heated, he'd either find himself filled with a passion that could be sated only by her, or she would seal away the words about to come pouring out of his mouth with her lips.

And then nothing else mattered but her.

God help him but he was in a bad way. Especially since he caught himself hoping more and more frequently that this pretense he found himself involved with would continue indefinitely—or at least until such time as he could figure out what was going on with him.

Closing the file, Dave looked at his watch. Damn it, it was getting late.

Ordinarily, the doors to the clinic would be closed by now and the number of people in the waiting area would be at least beginning to dwindle. But there was a new strain of flu making the rounds in Southern California. Children under ten seemed to be particularly susceptible to it, and it looked as if half the felled population were in the clinic's waiting room, most of them crying and growing more irritable.

Tonight was the night he'd told Kara he would take her out to that Chinese restaurant she liked in order to celebrate the donations her mother had rounded up. At first the invitation had been extended to her mother as well, but Paulette had demurred, saying three was a crowd.

"I will, however, let you bring back some of their absolutely fabulous shrimp lo mein for me," Paulette had told him.

"She wants proof we went" was Kara's cynical way of interpreting her mother's request.

He would have pointed out that it was a simple matter for him just to swing by the restaurant and get takeout without having to take her anywhere, but he knew when to keep things to himself. These days he picked his arguments, usually with an eye out for making up with her.

Now, from the looks of it, he was either going to have to give Kara a rain check on that dinner or wind up turning away at least half a dozen small, suffering patients and their equally suffering—although for an entirely different reason—mothers.

He made his choice. He was staying. But his nurse didn't have to, he thought. Approaching her, he said, "You can go home, Clarice."

The ebony-eyed, heavyset woman gave him one of her sterner looks and shook her head. "Don't go telling me what to do, Doctor Boy." She'd awarded him that affectionate nickname the first week he came and had been inundated with patients. She'd been forced to marvel at his staying power and had told him that he looked younger than her grandson, hence the nickname. "I can stick it out if you can."

He should have known better than to try to get her

to leave. "Thanks, Clarice. Tell the patient's mother in room two I'll be right there. I have to make a call first."

Clarice raised an eyebrow. "Canceling a date?" she asked.

He didn't ask her how she knew.

"Just canceling an obligation," he told her, deliberately avoiding a direct answer.

Clarice looked at him as if she saw right through his evasive maneuver. "It's a date. Tell that pushy woman I said hi."

Someday, he thought as he pressed numbers on the keypad, there was going to have to be a whole branch of science devoted to the study of the female mind so men like him had a prayer of understanding it.

He counted the number of rings. On the fourth one, he heard Kara pick up. "Hello?"

She sounded confused, he thought. Had she forgotten about tonight? "Kara, this is Dave."

"I figured it would be—that's what it says on my caller ID. What's up?"

He heard noise in the background. Where was she? "I'm running late. Actually, I'm not sure if I can make it tonight. The waiting room's packed and I can't turn them away. There's no place else in the area they can go where they can be treated for free," he explained.

Rather than comment on his possible no-show for their date, she said, "Sounds like you're having a revolt in your waiting room."

He supposed that was probably what it had to sound like to her. "It's full of kids." It was a given that young patients didn't do well confined to one room for hours at a time.

"You really should have something to keep them occupied while they're waiting. It would be a lot easier on their parents, and it would also go a long way toward reducing the level of your noise pollution."

She had a point, he thought. He was here only one day a week and tended not to occupy his mind with what was or wasn't out in the waiting room. His only concern was the patient. "Maybe I'll use a small portion of those donations your mother managed to raise for the clinic to buy some toys."

He heard her laugh. Three weeks ago, he would have bristled at the sound, offended that she was laughing at him. Now, although it still might be what was happening, he no longer took offense so easily.

"Toys?" she echoed. He could envision her wide smile. Even seeing it in his mind's eye had an effect on his gut. It hit him dead center, creating its own little tidal wave. "You really are old-fashioned, aren't you?"

"What's so funny?" he wanted to know, and then, before she could answer, he stopped to listen more closely to the sound he was picking up. "What's all that noise I hear in the background?" Dave asked. If he didn't know any better, he would have said she was somewhere surrounded by kids. But she worked with adults, or at least overgrown kids in adult clothing. "Where are you?"

"Someplace where I can implement a solution for your problem."

He didn't have time for riddles. He had to get back to his patients—and then it hit him.

On a hunch, still holding the cell phone in his hand, Dave came out of the closet-size office he shared with the other doctors who volunteered their services the other days of the week. Walking into the waiting room, he discovered that Kara was there—had they arranged to meet at the clinic? He didn't think so. He was almost certain they'd agreed that he would pick her up at her apartment. But if that was the case...

Dave looked at Clarice, but the nurse just shrugged her very wide shoulders, silently conveying that she hadn't a clue what was happening out here.

Kara was surrounded by an army of short people, all eagerly watching her every move. That included dropping to her knees beside an orange plastic chair that appeared to be bolted onto the floor.

"What are you doing here?" he wanted to know. And why was she now snaking her way under that chair?

"In a minute," he heard her mumble in response.

Then he heard her grunt as she struggled to push a plug into the electrical outlet directly in front of the bolted chair. When she snaked her way back out again, Kara brushed off a layer of dust bunnies from the front of her tank top before she stood up.

Only then did he notice the gaming system on the magazine table—now completely devoid of any magazines—standing beside the orange chair. Above the system was a twenty-inch monitor. That was new. He looked from it to Kara, momentarily too stunned to adequately form his question.

"Okay," Kara announced. He was about to ask her, "Okay, what?" when he realized she wasn't talking to him. She was talking to the squadron of pint-size patients who were still in the waiting room. "This is up and running," she told the children. Pointing to the four control pads, each in a different color, she said, "Four of you can play the game at the same time." She raised her eyes to Dave. "That should take care of your noise problem," she told him cheerfully.

That was when he saw that there was a different system hooked up across the room from the first one. The four hand controllers attached to that system were quickly claimed and four patients began their mighty adventure, all struggling to keep their colorful vehicles on the track while they raced toward a virtual finish line. The children not fast enough to grab a controller gathered around them, watching and waiting for their turn at the game.

Satisfied that the children were all occupied and no longer restless, bored and whiny, Kara finally turned around to face Dave. "I think I just might have found a solution to your noise-level problem *and* your restless-child syndrome," she told him with a very pleased grin on her lips.

"Good thing your mother secured those donations when she did," he commented. He knew that gaming systems didn't come cheaply. When he saw the way Kara frowned, he hadn't a clue what he could have said to bring that on. Or why the frown intensified when he asked, "So how much will I owe you?"

Forcing a smile back on her lips, she quipped. "Oh, so much more than you will ever be able to repay in one lifetime."

He hated being in anyone's debt—for any reason. "Seriously," he prodded.

Kara's smile was deliberately wide, deliberately innocent and deliberately bright. "Seriously," she echoed.

He tried again. "No, what do you want me to write on the check?"

"To Kara with love?" It was half a question, half a suggestion. The little girl standing beside her giggled and covered her mouth up with both hands. She muffled the sound but giggled again, her bright blue eyes dancing.

"Besides that," Dave said patiently, his pen poised over the checkbook he'd taken out of his back pocket.

"Be right back," she told the little girl she had begun tutoring on the game's finer points.

Taking Dave by the arm, she turned him around so that he was facing away from the people sitting out in the waiting room.

"Put your checkbook away," she ordered.

"But—" he began to protest. That was when he discovered that he really needed to talk quickly to get anything said around Kara when she was on a roll.

"Did I ask you for money?" she wanted to know, her eyes all but pinning him in place.

He was determined to get his piece out. "No, but this had to cost more than just two box tops and a stamp."

"I can see why you're regarded so highly in your profession. Nothing gets past you." She took a breath and he saw that she was not just looking for the right phrase, she was gathering herself together, as well. "Let me explain it to you so that even someone as removed from the lowly, common, everyday world as you obviously are can understand this. You did not ask me to bring any of these systems, thus you do not owe me anything for their sudden appearance at the clinic. You do *not* have to worry about footing this bill or any bill that has anything to do with video games."

She could see that his integrity was making him resist. Kara put her arm around his shoulders, or at least as high up as she could reach.

"The company I work for is producing video games for a certain target audience. Namely kids under fourteen. Once in a while, it's nice to come out into the real world and see that 'audience' play the games I've been slaving over. As a side benefit," she pointed out, gesturing toward first one group of kids, then the other, "it keeps them quiet for you." Stepping back, she smiled. "Consider it my contribution toward achieving world peace."

It wasn't that he wasn't grateful. It was just that he felt as if he'd been taken by storm. This was the way people in the path of a hurricane had to feel once it was over.

Dave shook his head. "Like I said, I'm never going to understand you."

She smiled broadly at him, obviously tickled by his admission. "It's what I'm counting on." She saw the puzzled look in his eyes. "Every woman likes to be considered mysterious," she explained, then winked.

There was mysterious, and then there was dealing with a complete enigma, he thought. Kara definitely fell into that second category. But he didn't have time to ponder over that. He had patients to see. Patients who, if he didn't start seeing them, were liable to be here all night, as would he.

And now that Kara was here, organizing his patients into two teams, he really didn't want to be here the rest of the night. There was dedication and then there was behavior bordering on the fanatical.

Maybe he would have slipped into that niche before, but now he had someone waiting for him who didn't need him to put a thermometer under her tongue. This might not actually be his life, but while it lasted it made one hell of a diversion.

Picking up a chart, he went to see his patient in the first exam room, already anticipating the light at the end of the tunnel. And, oddly enough, he knew that Kara would be standing there.

At least for now.

Chapter Fifteen

The end finally had a date pinned to it. It was coming tonight. At her mother's house right after dinner. Maybe even before.

She didn't much feel like eating. Kara wiped the sweat from her forehead with the back of her wrist. She was going to have to change clothes, she thought listlessly. She was practically soggy.

That's what happens when you sweat all day, she thought sarcastically. This had to be connected to her telling Dave that they were giving their final "lovebird" performance tonight. Her stomach had been in knots when she'd told him that last night, and he hadn't received the news very well.

Undoubtedly because he wanted to be the one to call the shots, she thought.

But this needed to happen. Now. It certainly couldn't

continue like this indefinitely. She needed to wrap this up, to bring it home.

Because the longer she put it off, the longer she waited before bringing an end to this mythical romance she and Dave were supposedly involved in, the harder that outcome was going to be to take. For her mother, for his mother and, damn it all to hell, for her, too, Kara thought irritably.

Feeling oddly woozy, she stopped getting ready for the fateful dinner and sat down on the edge of her bed. It was Friday night and she'd gotten home about half an hour ago. Usually that was enough time for her to get ready with time to spare, but tonight she was moving as if there were molasses in her veins. When she'd gotten up this morning, she'd felt off, and it had only worsened as the day progressed.

Damn Dave, anyway.

Against her own advice, against all reason, like a careless spider, she had gotten caught in her own web. And it didn't look as if she could work her way free without causing some damage.

What had possessed her to begin this stupid charade, anyway? If she'd held her peace, put up with her mother's annoying but heart-in-the-right-place, less-than-veiled hints and attempts to get her to jump into the dating field with both feet, then she would have never known that there was actually someone out there capable of rattling the very foundations of her world.

She also, Kara quietly reminded herself, wouldn't have gotten to know the teeth-jarring ecstasy Dave had introduced her to.

Makes it that much harder to do without it, she

thought, unable to shake the aura of sadness that insisted on descending over her.

"And next week's going to be harder than this week, Kara," she said aloud. "C'mon, you knew what you were getting into when you started all this. Don't get cold feet on me now."

The problem was that she *hadn't* known what she was getting into, not really. And right now, her feet were far from cold. They were hot.

All of her was hot.

Last night, she'd been so wrapped up in how and when to end this make-believe romance, she hadn't really paid attention to the fact that she was feeling progressively weaker and was now as energetic as a raccoon that'd been run over by a truck.

Flattened out and close to dead, she thought cynically.

Again she ran the back of her wrist along her forehead to wipe away fresh perspiration. Had she caught something the last time she'd gone to the clinic? On a generous roll, she'd gone to the clinic to bring a third gaming system and had stayed to hook it up. Her thought had been to minimize the possibility of squabbling children. This time, she'd noted, Clarice had actually smiled at her when she'd gotten the system up and running. The longtime nurse had given her personal seal of approval. It shouldn't have meant anything to her, Kara thought.

But it did.

Looking back, this was obviously a case of no good deed going unpunished because she *really* felt icky, not to mention dizzy.

When she heard a bell ringing, it took Kara a couple of moments to realize that the sound was coming from her own doorbell.

At least her ears weren't ringing, she thought.

Every bone in her body ached in protest as she got to her feet and dragged herself across the seemingly long distance from the foot of her bed to her front door.

Taking a deep breath, doing her best to pull herself together, she opened it. Dave was standing on the other side, looking far from happy, she noted dully.

He'd spent all day telling himself that he was going to welcome getting back to his usual routine. Welcome not seeing her anymore after tonight. And all the while, his mood kept darkening.

About to grumble a perfunctory greeting, the words died unspoken on his lips as Dave took a good look at the woman who had turned his world on its ear and was threatening now to drop-kick it to the curb.

Walking in, he told her, "You look like hell."

She left the door open and ambled into the living room, dropping onto the sofa. Her knees felt like rubber bands. *Used* rubber bands.

"Hello to you, too."

He doubled back to close the door, then crossed over to her. She really did look pretty awful. "What's going on?" he wanted to know.

Kara tried to shrug, but her shoulders suddenly weighed too much for her to complete the movement. Instead, she tried to content herself with giving him an accusing glare.

It was a feeble attempt.

She was definitely *not* comfortable in her own skin

tonight. It felt as if she were inhabiting someone else's body. And that body was sick.

"I think I caught something from one of your patients the last time I came to the clinic." Her breathing was growing progressively labored. "How come you don't come down with anything?"

Oh, but I have, Dave thought. *And for me, there's no medicine, no cure.*

But that wasn't anything he was about to share with her since she'd nonchalantly told him last night that it was time to finally put this little performance of theirs to bed. She'd undoubtedly have a sarcastic quip for him or, worse, laugh that he could have been dumb enough to get caught up in all this while she was only playacting.

So he merely cracked, "I don't know. Clean living, I guess." Concerned, he tried to put his hand to her forehead but she jerked her head back and almost fell over on the sofa as she did so. "Hold still," he ordered gruffly.

"Sorry, didn't mean to interfere with the latest scientific breakthrough for gauging a person's body temperature—or are you just trying to get fresh and working your way down?" Each word cost her a little and it took a great deal of effort to remain coherent. She didn't like this. She was hardly *ever* sick and she had no patience with her own weakness.

"Well, there's obviously nothing wrong with that rapier tongue of yours," he observed. "That still seems to be working just fine." He'd barely touched her forehead, but what he'd felt told him she was burning up. Her eyes appeared almost hollow with dark circles under them while the rest of her was very flushed. "You need to get into bed."

She lifted her chin, or thought she did. One hand on the sofa's arm for support, she pushed herself up to her feet, the picture of unsteady defiance. "Not even going to buy me dinner first?"

"I'm serious, Kara," he said sternly. "You're burning up. I don't know how you're managing to even stand." Although, he added silently, she was weaving in place a bit.

"Grit," she answered between clenched teeth. At this point, she could have sworn that the perspiration was pouring out of her.

"Either that, or you've glued yourself upright." Okay, enough was enough, he thought. Time to be her doctor and not her rejected would-be lover. He had an oath to follow. "In any case, you're going to bed."

"No, I'm not," she argued, although not with anywhere near the verve she'd intended. "We have a fight to get into, remember?" she protested. That *was* what they'd agreed to, wasn't it? To go to her mother's for dinner and then pick a ridiculous fight with one another that would escalate into a shouting match.

Oh God, her throat felt raw. How was she going to hurl accusations at him with a raw throat?

"I'd say we're already into it," he pointed out coolly. "Now, are you going to listen to me and go to bed, or are you going to force me to take drastic measures with you?"

"Sounds kinky," she quipped, doing her best to ignore the fact that her head was spinning at a progressively faster and faster speed. This didn't happen to her, she insisted. At least, it didn't happen without a soul-draining kiss from Dave to start her off.

She blinked, trying desperately to cast off the encroaching fog consuming her brain.

"You are the most infuriating woman," he complained. The next second, he scooped her up into his arms. Turning, he began to carry her into the bedroom.

"Where did the floor go?" she asked weakly. She was still trying to focus, though it was growing more and more difficult.

Beneath the barrage of sarcastic remarks was one very sick young woman, Dave thought. Her whole body felt hot in his arms, right through her clothing. That wasn't a good sign.

"How long have you been like this?" he asked her gruffly.

"About thirty years," she answered, pushing each word out. It took a great deal of effort. "My mother said I started talking when I was less than a year old."

He could readily believe that. And obviously, she hadn't learned how to stop since. "I mean, how long have you had this fever?"

She felt like she had been this way forever. She paused, trying to think.

"I woke up with it," she recalled. Lately, she'd been waking up with him beside her. But last night, after she'd told him about what they were going to do tonight, Dave had opted to leave. He didn't even bother making an excuse.

Oh well, that was something she was going to have to get used to from here on in, she'd told herself. She'd hated being alone in her bed, but that wasn't up for discussion. Ever. Though the fact remained that before this fever hit with full force she'd begun feeling remarkably empty and disconnected.

She knew it had to do with the fact that she was missing him—how stupid was that? How could she have gotten so used to having him there for her when she'd spent most of her life *not* having him there?

It made no sense.

Nothing made sense anymore. They were breaking up, she thought sadly.

"And you went to work?" It was more of an accusation than a question.

"It's what I do." The answer came out breathlessly. "Don't walk so fast," she ordered, doing her best to sound authoritative. The words came out in a raspy whisper. "You're making the room spin."

He was walking slow and in a straight line that couldn't be responsible for making *anything* spin. "What are you taking for your fever?" he asked, reaching her bedroom.

"I don't know." She pressed her cheek against his chest, seeking the comfort of hearing his heart beat. "What'll you give me?"

Well, at least her mind was still functioning, he consoled himself, even if it was an old joke.

With the side of his shoulder, he pushed the door open all the way and crossed to her bed. A bed, he couldn't help thinking, where so much had happened. A bed that, for a little while, had belonged to both of them.

Laying her down as gently as possible, Dave began to remove her tank top. It was soaking wet.

"No foreplay?" her voice croaked.

"I'll give you a rain check for the foreplay," he answered. "Right now I want you in bed, drinking lots of fluids. I'm also going to give you a shot of acetaminophen."

Every time she closed her eyes, the world kept insisting on fading and swirling around her. She was going to be sick.

She *was* sick, a little voice in her head reminded her. "I don't like the sound of that," she protested weakly.

It was a common enough medication, present in a weakened form in so many over-the-counter drugs. "It's to lower your fever," he told her. "It's faster than ingesting it."

She could barely make him out. The overhead lights kept blurring his features. "You just want an excuse to stick pins into me."

"Yeah, there's that, too." He knew that protesting or arguing with her would be extremely futile and get him nowhere except aggravated. "Stay here," he ordered. "I'll be right back."

She tried to prop herself up on her elbow and discovered that she barely had the strength to do so. Instead, she fell back, flat on her back. What was going on?

"Where...are...you...going?"

"To get my medical bag," he told her. "It's in the car."

"Oh." It took her a moment to process the information. "Are...we...going...to...play...doctor?"

"Something like that," he told her.

He really didn't like the way she looked. Up until now, this strain of flu attacked predominantly children and the elderly. But that didn't mean that everyone in between was safe. She obviously wasn't.

He returned in less than three minutes to find Kara exactly where he'd left her. That in itself wasn't a good sign. When had he ever known her to listen to common sense?

Worried, he quickly swabbed an area on her hip and then sank the needle completely into her flesh, dispensing the medication. He knew it was going to be painful.

Sure enough, her eyes flew open, a cry of protest rising to her lips.

"The fever should start going down soon," he promised her. Sitting on the edge of the bed, he took out his cell phone.

"Calling...for...backup?" she asked breathlessly.

"I'm calling your mother to tell her that we won't be there." He didn't want the woman worrying when they didn't show up.

Her eyes felt as if they were on fire. She closed them, unable to look at anything. "Don't...tell...her... I'm...sick," Kara begged weakly. "She'll...be...here with...chicken...soup." Struggling to stay conscious, she added, "She'll...worry... I...don't...want...her... to..." Her breathing was growing increasingly labored. Kara struggled to open her eyes again, but all she could manage were narrow slits. They shifted accusingly at him. "You...put...something...in...that...shot."

He *had* put in a little something extra. It was intended to make her sleep. "Only way I can have my way with you," he told her.

It was the last thing she heard before everything faded to black.

* * *

It figured, Dave thought as light slowly began to slip into Kara's bedroom, dutifully chasing away the shadows and sending night packing. Even a predominantly unconscious Kara was a handful to deal with.

She'd opened her eyes several times during the night, plying him with questions and heaping accusations on his head that told him she was hallucinating, skipping around in time.

And then there was that one instance...

Oh, he didn't doubt that her mind had been wandering then, and that her hold on reality had been weak. But hearing her, someone else would have sworn that she was at least *relatively* lucid.

He argued with himself, saying that she was ill and didn't really mean what had come out of her mouth at that point. But even so, he *really* had wanted Kara to mean it.

Delusional or not, he committed every word she'd uttered to memory. Because he wanted it to be true.

In the middle of tossing and turning on the bed, her eyes had suddenly flown open as her mouth was simultaneously engaged.

"I should have never started this. No, never started this," she told him with such feeling, for a second he thought she'd made some kind of miraculous recovery.

But then he realized that she was having a conversation she'd begun in her head. With him? With someone else? He had no way of knowing. But he intended to try to get as much as he could out of her.

"Started what?" he prodded. Exhausted, he'd stretched out on top of the covers and was lying next to her on the bed. He leaned in a little closer. Her voice was barely audible.

"This pretending thing with Dave. It's not pretending anymore," she admitted with a heartfelt sigh that went right through him.

Holding his breath, Dave asked, "Why not?"

"Because."

"Because why?" he pressed.

"Because I love him," she blurted out almost accusingly. Certainly not happily.

Hearing her, it was, he thought, not unlike the sensation a soldier might feel throwing himself on a grenade that was about to detonate and blow his buddies to kingdom come.

Dave could have sworn he felt the rumble going right through his entire body, mushrooming out from the center of his chest and reaching his fingertips and toes. Did she actually mean—?

Cautioning himself against getting caught up in all this, he broke in to say, "You what?"

"Love him," she repeated with effort, her voice fading even more. "I...love...Dave... And...he...hates me."

Busted! he thought, more pleased than he could recall ever being in his lifetime.

Out loud he did the best he could to comfort the young woman who'd once taken such glee in showing him that she was the "better man."

"No, he doesn't," he told her.

But his words, he saw, fell on deaf ears. She'd lapsed into unconsciousness again.

Up until that point, he'd grabbed only the slightest

of cat naps. After Kara had said what she had, unconscious or not, Dave found that he couldn't sleep at all.

So he lay beside her as dawn turned into morning,
replaying her words over and over again in his head.

She loved him. She'd said so. Drifting in and out
of consciousness, devoid of any inhibitions, she'd pro-
fessed her feelings. That was good enough for him.

Now, as he sat up, he looked at the still-sleeping
Kara and then slowly shook his head. Who would have
thought that he and Kara would *ever* be anything other
than a couple of squabbling acquaintances?

Rousing himself, he moved to the edge of the bed
and then came around to her side. She'd slept fitfully
for the most part, but even without a fever, she had a
tendency to move about the bed restlessly.

A moving target whether she was awake or asleep,
he thought, his mouth curving slightly.

She was right about the charade. If she'd never made
up her mind to undertake this fabricated romance to
teach their mothers a lesson, he might not have ever discovered that he could be moved to such heights, never
discovered that he had the capacity to feel so deeply.
In essence, being with Kara, making love with her, had
taken his black-and-white life and enhanced it with a
whole rainbow of colors.

So much so that he didn't think he could ever go
back to black and white again. He'd come too far.

In that respect, he thought as he got up and ran his
hand through his hair, she'd ruined him. Taken his life
and turned it upside down as well as inside out. The

tranquility he'd once treasured was no longer golden. It was boring. Everything was boring without Kara in it.

Who would have ever thought he'd be this happy about being ruined? Certainly not him.

And now, he knew, he was going to have to do something about it.

Chapter Sixteen

Her eyelids felt like lead.

Kara had been struggling to open her eyes for what felt like forever. It had really been only ten minutes, according to the clock on her nightstand, since she'd first pried them open only to have them shut on her immediately. But now she was really awake.

Or at least getting there.

It took her several seconds to orient herself and realize that she was in her bed in her room. She needed another couple of seconds to realize that it was daylight, which meant that she must have been out for a long time. The last thing she remembered was sitting on her sofa, feeling like death warmed over, and it had been evening.

She didn't exactly feel much stronger now, but at

least her brain was returning to the land of the living and actually working.

The first thing her brain did was let her know that she wasn't alone. Startled, it took her exactly one erratic heartbeat to recognize the owner of the back she was looking at.

Dave.

What was he doing here?

She vaguely remembered that he had come to pick her up last night. Hadn't he gone home? For the life of her, she couldn't remember if he did or not. Couldn't really remember much of anything beyond opening the door to let him in. Details after that felt as if they were lost in a fog.

"Don't you have a home to go to?" she asked, her voice sounding really raspy to her ear.

Surprised, Dave swung around. For a second, she thought she saw relief wash over his features, but then it was gone and he looked austere again. Or maybe still.

"Apparently I seem to like yours better." Crossing back to her, he put his hand to her forehead. It was cool for the first time since he'd arrived. The worst of it seemed to be over, he thought. Even her cheeks weren't as pink as they had been. "Looks as if your fever finally broke."

A few vague memories floated through the back edges of her mind. She remembered he'd looked concerned. "Have you been here the whole time?"

"Yes."

Hadn't they agreed to stage the breakup last night? He was supposed to be out of her life, not hovering over her. She didn't get it. "Why?"

Feelings, especially his own, had never been something he could easily talk about. Dave shrugged. "I had nothing else scheduled after you canceled on dinner at your mother's."

She recalled being dizzy and feeling hot all over. "I didn't exactly cancel," she protested.

"No," he agreed. "You're right. What you did was pass out." A small smile curved his mouth.

"My mother," she remembered suddenly, replaying some of his words in her head.

He was way ahead of her. "Was duly notified and gently instructed to refrain from arriving here with a pot of chicken soup."

Kara's eyebrows drew together in a confused line. "Why would you do that?"

She really had no recollection of last night, did she? "Because you asked me to."

She shook her head. Nothing was really coming together in her mind yet. It was all just disjoined pieces bobbing up and down. "I don't remember saying that to you."

He looked at her for a long moment. A semismile barely passed over his lips and then receded as if it had never been there at all.

"You probably don't remember saying a lot of things to me."

Kara stiffened. There was something about the way he said that that made the hairs on the back of her neck stand up. The rest of her felt as if it had just been put on red alert.

"Like what?" she asked in a hushed tone.

"Things," he replied vaguely. "No need to go into them now."

Just the way he said it, she knew she needed to find out what she'd said.

"Tell me," she insisted.

His eyes held hers for a moment, and she felt her stomach take a dive off the high board. "You really want to go into this now?"

Oh God, he was daring her to ask. This had to be worse than she thought. But what could she have told him and not remembered? She would have happily believed he was bluffing just to get under her skin, but she knew him. He didn't bluff. There wasn't going to be any peace for her until she knew what he *thought* he knew.

"Yes," she breathed. "Tell me. Now. Please," she added in case he was waiting for her to humble herself.

The smile on his lips went clear down to her bones. She braced herself.

"You told me you loved me."

She wasn't braced nearly enough, she realized as every system within her screamed, *Mayday! Mayday! Damage control!*

She grabbed at the first excuse she could. "I was delirious," she pointed out so quickly, he almost got whiplash.

The smile on his lips told her he knew better. "You were uninhibited," he corrected. Before she could protest, he put the tip of his finger to her lips to still them and made his case. "To the casual observer, you don't seem to be uptight and repressed, but it turns out that you really are. At least as far as your feelings are concerned." And he, Dave thought, could fully relate to that.

The best defense, her father had always told her, was a good offense. So she forged ahead, although not nearly with as much verve as she would have liked. "I wouldn't throw rocks if I were you."

"No rock throwing," Dave assured her. "I'm just making a very logical observation. Why is that, do you think?"

"That you think you're being logical?" she asked him with a dismissive sniff. "I'm sure I haven't the faintest idea."

"No," he said patiently, "I'm asking you why you're afraid to let your feelings out, afraid to let anyone know that you even *can* feel." He took his best guess. "Someone walk out on you, Kara?"

She resented his probing. Resented, even more, his hitting so close to the truth. "Since when did you become a shrink?"

"Since when did you become afraid of a straight answer?" he countered.

She'd had enough of this. Throwing back the covers, she was about to storm out of bed and the room, praying her knees wouldn't buckle under her, when her plan was instantly aborted.

She had nothing on beneath the blanket.

Stunned, she threw the blanket back into place, anchoring it down with her arms, and glared at him accusingly. "You took off my clothes."

There was a reason for that. "You were sopping wet," he explained.

Why would she be sopping wet? "What did you do to me?" she demanded.

He gave her a quick summary. "I gave you an injection to break the fever. You were perspiring so much your clothes were almost soaked right through. All I did was get you out of your wet clothes."

He made it sound completely altruistic. "And nothing else?" she asked suspiciously.

"I applied a few wet compresses to your forehead, but the shot did most of the work. And as for what you're implying, tempting though you might look to me, I prefer you awake if I'm going to be doing anything that requires tacit consent."

Her heart believed him. Her mind was having trouble. Especially in light of the expression on his face. "You're smirking," she accused.

It was always going to be like this, he thought. A constant battle, heated or otherwise. And now he understood what had been missing from those other relationships that never went beyond a few steps. Passion. Passion had been missing. All those other women had been too much like him, too orderly, too blandly agreeable. They were black-and-white, and Kara, incessantly argumentative Kara, was the rainbow that he subconsciously craved.

"No, I'm not. That's called a smile," he informed her.

A smile at her expense, Kara thought. Because, temporarily out of her head, she'd blurted out her true feelings.

She tried another approach. "I can't be held responsible for anything I said when I was ill," she protested.

When he said nothing, some of her ardor slipped away. "You were really here the whole night?"

He nodded. "Yes, I was." And then he added, "And the next day, as well."

She stared at him, utterly stunned. "The next— How long have I been out?"

He looked at his watch before answering, "A little less than thirty-six hours."

"Thirty—six—" No, that had to be wrong. "You're just making that up," she protested.

"I could carry you into the living room, put on the news channel. They always run the time and the date in the lower right-hand corner of their broadcast." He rose to his feet as if he was going to pick her up and make good on his suggestion. Upset over losing a day, Kara waved him back. She couldn't remember when she'd ever slept so long.

"I believe you."

He laughed shortly. "Nice to hear you're that trusting."

She wasn't accustomed to his sounding like that. "Sarcasm doesn't become you."

"Sorry." He inclined his head. "Didn't mean to invade your home territory."

She deserved that, she supposed. He'd been nothing but kind and obviously caring even if she'd been out for most of it, and as a reward for his behavior, she was being combative.

But, in her defense, she wasn't used to being the one who needed help. "Why did you do it, Dave?" she asked.

He wasn't sure exactly what part she was referring to. "Do what?"

"Why did you stay here with me? You could have just put me into bed and left me there."

Did she really think that? "You were sick, I'm a doctor. It's kind of self-explanatory." Not to mention that she had "thoughtfully" gotten sick on a Friday night. That afforded him the weekend to watch over her.

"No, it's not. Most doctors would have called a family member, or, if the person was really sick, they would have called an ambulance and had the person taken to a hospital." This was definitely above and beyond the call of duty.

This, she realized, was something a friend did for another friend. *Or a lover,* a little voice whispered in her head.

"I'd rather not have you haunting my hospital," he quipped.

That was the kind of flippant thing she would have said to him. Kara picked at the sheet, pulling it in tighter around herself. She kept her eyes down as she asked, "I really said...you know?"

"Yes, you really said 'you know,'" he confirmed, amused.

Kara blew out a breath. "I'm surprised you're still here, then." He looked at her, puzzled. "Hearing something like that from me, I would have expected you to run for the hills."

"Why?" he asked. "Love shouldn't make a man run. Your mouth, on the other hand, well, that's another story." He paused for a moment. He had nothing to lose by pushing this and hopefully everything to gain if she stopped playing games and told him the truth. "Why are you so afraid of love, Kara?"

"I'm not afraid of love," she denied indignantly with a toss of her head. She instantly regretted the latter.

"You're also not much of a liar," he observed. "I'm waiting."

It was on the tip of her tongue to tell him he could wait until hell froze over, but she knew him well enough to know he would. And besides, he didn't deserve that. Not after he'd been so selfless.

So, with a sigh, she answered his question. It wasn't easy. "When my father died, I saw my mother all but completely fall apart. I was never so scared in my life."

He could well imagine. "But she didn't, did she?" he pointed out.

"No, but—" That wasn't the point. The point was the horror her mother had felt. The horror of being left behind to live, to take one step after the other, in a world that no longer contained the man she loved. The *only* man she'd ever love.

"And she has her memories of life with your father, doesn't she?" Dave continued.

"Yes," she grudgingly admitted. And then her eyes widened as she looked at him. "Are you going to tell me that 'it's better to have loved and lost than never to have loved at all'?" He wouldn't even dare think about that now, she silently threatened.

His broad shoulders rose and fell in a careless shrug. "Alfred, Lord Tennyson seemed to think so," he told her. "Who are we to disagree?"

That was all well and good in poetry, but this was

real life. And real life brought with it scars. "I don't want to ache the way my mother ached."

"She ached because she'd loved. There are far worse things than death," he told her.

She couldn't imagine there being something worse to endure than the death of a loved one. "Such as?" she challenged.

"Being alone," he told her simply. Being alone the way he'd been alone—until she returned to his life. That was when he came to understand what he'd been missing all along. Her. "There are no guarantees in life, and no one lives forever." He looked at her and knew that there was only one way to play this. It was all or nothing. He didn't usually take risks, but then that was why his life was all but flat-lining. It was time to take that risk. "All I can do is promise to love you for the rest of my life."

She had to be hearing things. "You love me?" Kara asked incredulously.

Why did she look so surprised? He would have thought that she at least suspected as much. "That didn't occur to you? Say, around the second time we made love?"

Why would she have thought that? Unless, of course, he thought she was that naive. "Men don't have to *be* in love to *make* love," she told him.

"Granted. And God knows I didn't want to be, not with you," he told her honestly. "But I don't seem to have a choice in this."

She was still very much stuck in first gear—afraid to believe what her heart *wanted* to believe. "You love me?" she repeated, mystified.

"I thought we already established that." He smiled. Okay, this was for the record. "Yes, I love you. And I'd like to keep on loving you. I stopped pretending two days into this charade and finally admitted that little fact to myself. Now, you can take your time making up your mind how you feel—"

It was beginning to sink in, but she was still afraid to embrace the thought. "Hey, with medical care costing what it does these days, I'd be a fool to turn down the opportunity to have my very own doctor on call 24/7."

His eyes pinned her down. "And that's the only reason?"

"No, it's not the only reason." She sighed. "You already know I love you," she said, staring down at the comforter. She felt more naked than she had when she'd thrown the comforter back. This admission left her completely exposed. It wasn't a position she relished.

He ran his fingertips along her cheek, sending butterflies into both their stomachs. "I'm going to need you to convince me a little more when you're feeling stronger."

"Whoa, feel that?" she cried.

"Feel what?" he asked, puzzled.

Her eyes teased his. "My strength. That was my strength, coming back." She put her arms out to him, and he took her into his own. "You know what this means, don't you?"

He was a little wary of giving her an answer. With Kara he never knew what was safe and what played right into her hands. "What?"

"That our mothers were right. About matching us

up." She rolled her eyes. "They're going to be impossible to live with from now on."

He grinned, brushing a strand of hair back from her face. "I wasn't planning on living with them."

The way he left that open had her asking, "Who are you planning on living with?"

He looked into her eyes and wondered why he hadn't seen this before. But then, maybe he had. Maybe he'd been aware of this all along and that was why he never became involved with anyone else.

"You."

There went her heart again. Going off like fireworks on the Fourth of July. "You want to move in together?" she questioned, surprised. "Isn't that a big step for you?" She knew how cautious he was, how much he liked his own space. And here he was, asking her to share that space with him. Did it get any better than this?

"That's the usual step two people take after getting married."

"Married?" It did, it really did get better than this, she thought—provided she wasn't hallucinating. "I think my fever's back."

"Well, then I'll just have to nurse you back to health again." He brushed his lips against her forehead. Just as he thought. It was cool.

Kara was staring at him, wide-eyed. Trying to absorb what he was saying to her. Afraid to take it to heart and yet, she knew she already had. "You're serious."

"I'm a doctor," he told her innocently. "Making people healthy is what I do."

"Idiot," she cried. He knew perfectly well what she was referring to. "I'm talking about asking me to marry you." She pinned him down in earnest, putting the question to him. "You're asking me?"

He nodded. "I'm asking you."

She didn't want him parroting her. "I want the words, Dave. I want to hear the words. The official words." She held her breath, her eyes on his lips.

"Kara Calhoun, will you marry me and keep turning my boring life upside down?" His eyes crinkled at the very end.

Oh God, he was really asking her. *Really* asking her. It was all she could do to keep from screaming out the single word. Her eyes danced as she said, "Well, if you put it that way—yes!"

He let go of the breath he'd been holding. Kara was nothing if not unpredictable.

"We're going to have to tell our mothers," he reminded her.

"I know. How about right after the first baby?" she suggested, entwining her arms around his neck. "Until then, we can just keep it a secret."

He knew she didn't mean it, or at least *thought* she didn't mean it. But it cost him nothing to go along with it.

"Works for me," he murmured just before they sealed the bargain with a very long kiss.

It occurred to Kara, just before she sank into the kiss, that she'd had her last first kiss that evening right after the birthday party.

Her feeling of contentment and joy knew no bounds. She was counting on it remaining that way for the next fifty years or so.

Epilogue

"So was I right, or was I right?" Paulette Calhoun asked smugly as she adjusted her baby-blue dress, her eyes meeting her best friend's in the mirror.

Lisa Scarlatti shifted slightly in the limited space right outside the room where the bride was getting ready. Technically this was a room, too, but someone was going to have to show her the floor plans before she was convinced of that.

She paused, allowing her best friend to have her moment. After all, it *had* been her idea that had started this wonderful ball rolling. "Doesn't leave me much of a choice, does it, Mother of the Bride?"

Paulette turned, her blue dress brushing against the mint-green one Lisa had on. "There doesn't really need to be a choice, Mother of the Groom, does there?"

"Go ahead, gloat." Lisa laughed softly. "You have every right to."

Paulette inclined her head. "Thank you. I fully intend to, and yes, I know." She took a deep breath after glancing in the narrow mirror one last time. "Well, I'm ready—how about you?"

Lisa's smile was radiant. "I've been ready for this for the last thirty years."

"Thirty?" Paulette echoed. "Dave's thirty-two."

"I decided not to push the first two years," Lisa deadpanned.

"Very understanding of you."

They entered the next room together, and the moment Paulette saw her daughter, she felt her eyes begin to sting. Kara was in her wedding dress and had just put on her veil.

"Oh God," Paulette moaned, taking out her handkerchief, "I told myself I wasn't going to cry."

"Mother, don't you dare." The words were half a warning, half a plea. It wasn't as if her mother hadn't seen the dress on her before. She'd been there for the last fitting and had helped her with it just this morning.

"She's right," Lisa told her best friend. "Tears are contagious." As if to prove it, she dabbed at her own eyes, which had become moist. "So don't cry."

"I won't," Paulette promised, even as another tear spilled onto her cheek.

Kara shook her head, then readjusted her veil. "You're hopeless, Mother."

Paulette came closer. *It was happening. It was finally happening.* "And you are the most beautiful sight I have ever seen."

"Think Dave will think so?" Kara asked as she examined her reflection in the mirror one last time. Her floor-length gown nipped in at the waist, then flowed out with yards of satin and lace. The strapless bodice had delicate beadwork woven all through it.

"If he doesn't, he's no son of mine," Lisa assured her.

Just then, there was a knock on the door, followed by a deep voice asking. "Everything all right in there? It's almost time to make this official."

"Dave!" Kara cried, pleasure and relief in her voice. There was a small part of her that had been afraid he'd change his mind at the very last minute and make his escape, taking off for parts unknown. But he hadn't. He was here. Her smile widened.

Horrified that her son might come in, Lisa quickly opened the door a crack and angled her body through the space. Once outside, she firmly shut the door again, blocking access with her own slender body.

"Dave, don't take this the wrong way, but go away!" she ordered. She tugged on her son's arm to lead him away from the door. "It's bad luck for the groom to see the bride before the wedding."

His smile was tolerant as he looked at his mother. He owed her a lot and he knew it. "Then I'll just go to the altar and wait for her there." He raised his voice so that Kara could hear him through the door. "I'll be the impatient guy in the black tuxedo next to the priest."

"I'll be sure to look for you," Kara called out.

A moment later, strains of the wedding march began to filter into the small room.

"They're playing your song, darling," Paulette told her daughter.

Kara took a deep breath. "Okay, here we go," she murmured, suddenly feeling butterflies in her stomach. "Just promise me something, Mother."

Paulette squeezed her daughter's hand as more tears slid down her cheeks. "Anything."

Kara opened the door. The music swelled. "Promise me that you two won't start playing matchmakers with your grandchildren until they're at least in their twenties."

"Well, I won't," Paulette promised solemnly as they left the little room. "But I'm afraid I really can't speak for Lisa...."

* * * * *

HEART & HOME

Heartwarming romances where love can
happen right when you least expect it.

◈ Harlequin®
SPECIAL EDITION®

COMING NEXT MONTH
AVAILABLE MARCH 27, 2012

#2179 A COLD CREEK REUNION
The Cowboys of Cold Creek
RaeAnne Thayne

#2180 THE PRINCE'S SECRET BABY
The Bravo Royales
Christine Rimmer

#2181 FORTUNE'S HERO
The Fortunes of Texas: Whirlwind Romance
Susan Crosby

#2182 HAVING ADAM'S BABY
Welcome to Destiny
Christyne Butler

#2183 HUSBAND FOR A WEEKEND
Gina Wilkins

**#2184 THE DOCTOR'S NOT-SO-LITTLE
SECRET**
Rx for Love
Cindy Kirk

REQUEST YOUR FREE BOOKS!

2 FREE NOVELS PLUS 2 FREE GIFTS!

◆ Harlequin®

SPECIAL EDITION

Life, Love & Family

YES! Please send me 2 FREE Harlequin® Special Edition novels and my 2 FREE gifts (gifts are worth about $10). After receiving them, if I don't wish to receive any more books, I can return the shipping statement marked "cancel." If I don't cancel, I will receive 6 brand-new novels every month and be billed just $4.49 per book in the U.S. or $5.24 per book in Canada. That's a saving of at least 14% off the cover price! It's quite a bargain! Shipping and handling is just 50¢ per book in the U.S. and 75¢ per book in Canada.* I understand that accepting the 2 free books and gifts places me under no obligation to buy anything. I can always return a shipment and cancel at any time. Even if I never buy another book, the two free books and gifts are mine to keep forever.

235/335 HDN FEGF

Name	(PLEASE PRINT)

Address	Apt. #

City	State/Prov.	Zip/Postal Code

Signature (if under 18, a parent or guardian must sign)

Mail to the **Reader Service:**
IN U.S.A.: P.O. Box 1867, Buffalo, NY 14240-1867
IN CANADA: P.O. Box 609, Fort Erie, Ontario L2A 5X3

Not valid for current subscribers to Harlequin Special Edition books.

Want to try two free books from another line?
Call 1-800-873-8635 or visit www.ReaderService.com.

* Terms and prices subject to change without notice. Prices do not include applicable taxes. Sales tax applicable in N.Y. Canadian residents will be charged applicable taxes. Offer not valid in Quebec. This offer is limited to one order per household. All orders subject to credit approval. Credit or debit balances in a customer's account(s) may be offset by any other outstanding balance owed by or to the customer. Please allow 4 to 6 weeks for delivery. Offer available while quantities last.

Your Privacy—The Reader Service is committed to protecting your privacy. Our Privacy Policy is available online at www.ReaderService.com or upon request from the Reader Service.

We make a portion of our mailing list available to reputable third parties that offer products we believe may interest you. If you prefer that we not exchange your name with third parties, or if you wish to clarify or modify your communication preferences, please visit us at www.ReaderService.com/consumerschoice or write to us at Reader Service Preference Service, P.O. Box 9062, Buffalo, NY 14269. Include your complete name and address.

HSE11B

Taft Bowman knew he'd ruined any chance he'd had for happiness with Laura Pendleton when he drove her away years ago...and into the arms of another man, thousands of miles away. Now she was back, a widow with two small children...and despite himself, he was starting to believe in second chances.

Harlequin Special® Edition® presents a new installment in USA TODAY bestselling author RaeAnne Thayne's miniseries,
THE COWBOYS OF COLD CREEK.

Enjoy a sneak peek of
A COLD CREEK REUNION

Available April 2012 from Harlequin® Special Edition®

A younger woman stood there, and from this distance he had only a strange impression, as though she was somehow standing on an island of calm amid the chaos of the scene, the flashing lights of the emergency vehicles, shouts between his crew members, the excited buzz of the crowd.

And then the woman turned and he just about tripped over a snaking fire hose somebody shouldn't have left there.

Laura.

He froze, and for the first time in fifteen years as a firefighter, he forgot about the incident, his mission, just what the hell he was doing here.

Laura.

Ten years. He hadn't seen her in all that time, since the week before their wedding when she had given him back his ring and left town. Not just town. She had left the whole damn country, as if she couldn't run far enough to get away from him.

Some part of him desperately wanted to think he had made some kind of mistake. It couldn't be her. That was just some other slender woman with a long sweep of honey-blond hair and big, blue, unforgettable eyes. But no. It was definitely Laura. Sweet and lovely.

Not his.

He was going to have to go over there and talk to her. He didn't want to. He wanted to stand there and pretend he hadn't seen her. But he was the fire chief. He couldn't hide out just because he had a painful history with the daughter of the property owner.

Sometimes he hated his job.

Will Taft and Laura be able to make the years recede...or is the gulf between them too broad to ever cross?

Find out in
A COLD CREEK REUNION
Available April 2012 from Harlequin® Special Edition®
wherever books are sold.

Celebrate the 30th anniversary
of Harlequin® Special Edition® with a bonus story
included in each Special Edition® book in April!

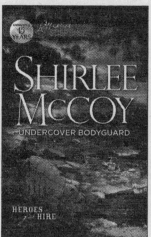